PRAISE FOR LEON GARFIELD

Leon Garfield's stories are a rich and highly flavored stir-fry of eighteenth-century adventure. Under their wild story lines the books reveal an impressive knowledge of Victorian and Regency lowlife. Young readers are drawn in by the involved, mysterious plots, adults appreciate the black, sometimes outrageous humor. These are books for communal family reading, in the way that Dickens and Fielding were enjoyed by parents and children together in the nineteenth century. It is a fine thing that Leon Garfield's rip-roaring and funny tales should be brought back into circulation for a new generation of readers.   —*Joan Aiken*

Leon Garfield is unmatched for sheer, exciting storytelling; and, as well, for grand style and spirit. He has a perfect eye for character and a perfect ear for language. Whether suspenseful, droll, or deeply moving—or all this at the same time—his books are rich in color, bursting with vitality. He writes in the great tradition of English literature but his voice is uniquely his own. The reader simply can't stop reading him—and the rewards are magnificent.

—*Lloyd Alexander*

I envy any reader discovering Leon Garfield. He's a wonderful storyteller!   —*Nancy Bond*

Leon Garfield was an inspired storyteller whose exuberant novels remind us of the unrivaled pleasures of reading. A brilliant stylist, Garfield was also a masterful plotter, whose novels are filled with mystery, secrets, surprises, and some of the most memorable characters since Dickens. Though chiefly set in the eighteenth century, his novels are timeless in their thematic treatment of good and evil and in their capacity to delight, stimulate, and satisfy. Leon Garfield's name belongs on everybody's shortlist of truly great writers for readers of all ages. —*Michael Cart*

Open a Leon Garfield novel and you'll be powerless until you've finished it. Nobody has ever equalled his glorious bloodcurdling mix of suspense, humor, and hypnotic storytelling.

—*Susan Cooper*

If James Bond were a twelve-year-old boy living in eighteenth-century England, his life of surprise and danger and self-discovery might have been recorded by Leon Garfield, just as he has brilliantly recorded the adventures of *Smith*, Bartholomew in *Black Jack*, and his other courageous and appealing young heroes.

—*Alison Lurie*

Some writers specialize in nifty plotting, learning from the movies how to pace a story like a foxhunt, a tiger chase. Some writers are noteworthy for the gleam and tension of their excellently wrought prose. Some writers relish building into their stories a dark and potent moral born, if we readers are lucky, of an uncompromising worldview. Few writers deliver all of the above. Leon Garfield does. He was head and shoulders above his contemporaries. He remains a talent to be remembered and a master to be emulated. Turn the pages fast, to gulp down the story; then start back at the beginning, to cherish the storytelling. —*Gregory Maguire*

There has never been a writer to equal Garfield for ebullient, rip-roaring, gruesome, joyful, and witty evocation of the past, and for wonderful page-turning adventure stories. When is Garfield's past? You can't exactly place it—then as his tales unfold you understand that in his hands the past is a golden lantern, lighting up for us with penetrating tenderness and laughter and deep understanding the present and eternal nature of the human heart.

—*Jill Paton Walsh*

Born well into the twentieth century, Leon Garfield was the last great nineteenth-century author. Hooves rang on the paving stones of Dickens's London in Leon Garfield's mind. And he had the heart of a lamplighter, throwing and dispelling shadows. He handed the past to his readers because he never seemed to be looking back. Research? Undoubtedly, but something in his heart remembered.   —*Richard Peck*

Leon Garfield's vivid descriptions and dialog transported me almost bodily into 18th-century England with characters as fully realized as the period and setting. Reissuing Leon Garfield's novels is a great gift to lovers of story of all ages.

—*Suzanne Fisher Staples*

Of all the talents that emerged in the field of British writing for children in the 1960s, that of Leon Garfield seems to me to be the richest and strangest. I am tempted to go on and say that his stories are the tallest, the deepest, the wildest, the most spine-chilling, the most humorous, the most energetic, the most extravagant, the most searching, the most everything.   —*John Rowe Townsend*

JOHN DIAMOND

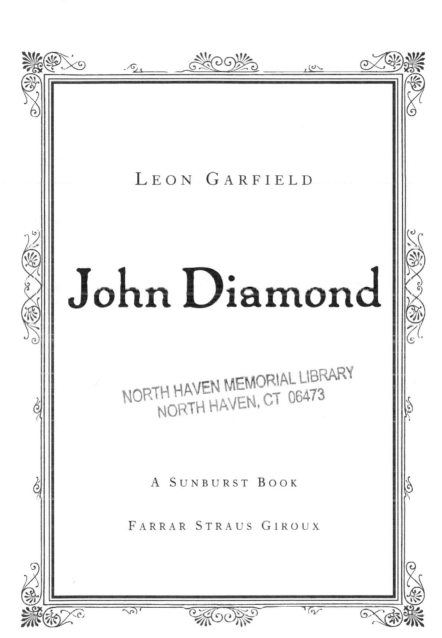

LEON GARFIELD

John Diamond

A SUNBURST BOOK

FARRAR STRAUS GIROUX

Library of Congress Cataloging-in-Publication Data
Garfield, Leon.
    John Diamond / Leon Garfield.— Farrar, Straus and Giroux ed.
        p.   cm.
    Summary: Unsettling words from his dying father set twelve-year-old William
on a mission to eighteenth-century London where, in the course of searching for
his father's mysterious business partner Alfred Diamond, he encounters an odd
assortment of characters, some of whom seem determined to kill him.
    ISBN 0-374-42441-1 (pbk.)
    [1. Mystery and detective stories—Fiction.   2. Adventure and adventurers—Fiction.
3. Fathers and sons—Fiction.   4. London (England)—History—18th century—
Fiction.   5. Great Britain—History—18th century—Fiction.]   I. Title.

PZ7.G17943 Jo   2001
    [Fic]—dc21   00-34132

To Vivien

JOHN DIAMOND

I

I OUGHT TO BEGIN with the footsteps; but first of all I must tell you that my name is William Jones and that I was twelve years old when I began to hear them.

I have two older sisters, Cissy and Rebecca, and a mother who was born a Turner, and I have an Uncle Turner to prove it.

But the story is about my father, chiefly.

He was a tall, handsome man, with his own hair, his own teeth, and, in fact, with nothing false about him.

I think he was rather proud of his appearance, and not a little ashamed to have a son who wore his clothes like a footpad and tied a cravat as if he'd been badly hanged. Those, by the way, were his words; but not in public as I was, after all, his son.

I was born in Woodbury, a village about two miles from the town of Hertford, where I went to school. We lived in a fine old house with a great many passages and winding stairs and surprising windows; and we kept our own coach. Although my Uncle Turner would not allow that we were rich, we were certainly in easy circumstances.

My father made his fortune in London. He'd been in coffee—

not like a spoon, but in the way of buying and selling it, in barrels and sacks. He never talked about his years in trade, which consequently gave them an air of mystery and romance, with a strong sensation of ships.

He never really talked much at all; or at least, not to me, except to remark on my dirty fingernails and to ask me if I intended to grow up to be a sorrow to my mother and a disgrace to my sisters, who always nodded as if they fully expected that to be the case.

Yet, like everybody else, I couldn't help liking and admiring him, and would have done anything to earn his praise. I would lie awake at nights, dreaming of distinguishing myself in every possible way—except, of course, the one that would have pleased him most, which was to be clean, neat and studious, to follow in his footsteps and be a pillar of the community.

His footsteps! Now I've come to them. I hated and dreaded them. Every night I heard them, back and forth, back and forth across his room, which was directly under mine.

They started when the house was quiet, at about midnight, and went on and on until I fell asleep. Sometimes I tried to count them, like sheep, and then to work out how far they would have reached if they'd been laid end to end. I think it was to Edinburgh; but later I discovered that his journey was a good deal longer.

At first I thought he might have had the toothache; but, as his face was never swollen, and he had no trouble with eating, it was plain that the reason lay deeper than that.

I knew he was unwell. Dr. Fisher from Hertford had called to see him several times, and had gone away looking glum; so it occurred to me that, just as some people have the sleeping sickness, some the falling sickness, my father had the walking sickness, and that was the cause of it.

If so, it was a very strange malady, for it only attacked him by night and drove him from his bed, to walk and walk, as if he would wear out a grave in the floorboards with his feet.

That he was as ill as that—to bring graves to mind, I mean—I first learned from Mrs. Alice one Saturday afternoon in September, when the rain had kept me in.

Mrs. Alice was our cook and housekeeper rolled tightly into one, and secured by an enormous white apron and a crusty white cap, so that she looked like a wrinkled old baby who had been left waiting at the font.

I was in the scullery, helping myself to raisin wine, which was kept in a stone jug covered with a bit of beaded muslin to prevent the flies.

She came in so suddenly that I had no chance to escape and could only stand, with the jug up to my face and the muslin veil on my head, waiting for her to shout loud enough for my father to hear.

Instead, she gazed at me mournfully and said it was high time I stopped thinking only about myself and began to think of being a support to my mother and sisters as my father could not live forever.

Much relieved that she hadn't lost her temper, I put down the jug and attempted to depart. She stood in my way and said, even more mournfully, that she hoped I prayed for my father every night as I'd never forgive myself if I was to wake up one morning and find that it was too late.

"Too late for what, Mrs. Alice?"

"Never you mind," said she. "It's not my place to tell you. But soon enough you'll have to know."

As she said this, she looked up at the scullery ceiling very meaningfully, as if we had angels in the house, like bailiffs, and she didn't want them to hear.

She wouldn't say any more; and, in response to my plaguing her, only shook her head and repeated:

"Never you mind."

But I did mind. In fact I was deeply frightened and somehow got the idea that I was to blame and that my father was dying of a worthless son, and sooner or later it would be diagnosed as such by Dr. Fisher.

I lay awake at night, listening to the footsteps below in utter terror, and wondering what I would do if they were to stop suddenly and that I alone, in all the house, would know that my father was dead and that I had done it.

In a perfect agony of remorse, I prayed for him and did everything I could, in the way of cleanliness and behavior, to improve myself and undo the harm that, apparently, I had done. But the walking went on and on; and, worse than ever, began to be accompanied by deep, unearthly sighs.

I said nothing about it to anyone, partly because I thought I might have been to blame, and partly because it was something between him and me—a secret that we shared.

Some time in November, my father took a turn for the worse. He began to go downhill so rapidly that it was as if he himself had been taken by surprise, and had slipped, and left a good part of his substance behind. Overnight, it seemed, he became horribly thin and bloodless, so that even his fingernails were as white as paper.

He didn't go outside anymore, chiefly, I think, because his clothes looked so ill upon him, and he was ashamed to be a scarecrow. Dr. Fisher came to see him almost every day, and there sprang up, on the table by his bed, a whole forest of green glass medicine bottles that jingled, when you went in, like tiny frantic bells.

Once Dr. Fisher brought a nurse with him, a Mrs. Small. She was a gaunt-looking widow from Hertford who had buried three husbands (her own, I think), "on account of the aggravation of leaves."

I'm sure she said "leaves," but I never discovered how it had come about—whether by the leaves dropping into their beer and poisoning it, or by straight suffocation—as Mrs. Alice looked up, and, seeing me agog at the kitchen door, said:

"Ssh! Mrs. Small! Little pitchers, little pitchers!"

At once Mrs. Small stared at me with great hostility, and, compressing her lips, refused to utter another word until I had gone.

Soon after, I saw her bustling down the drive in the wake of Dr. Fisher, and pausing to make little darts and flurries at her archenemies, as they floated down from the trees near the house.

Dr. Fisher had wanted her to stay behind and look after my father, and my mother had been in agreement; but my father wouldn't hear of it. I suspected it was because he was frightened that Mrs. Small would spy on him and find out about his walking by night.

Dr. Fisher brought her back for a second time, but by then—it was nearly at the end of November—my father had worked himself into such a state of secrecy, that he could hardly bear to have anybody at all in the room with him.

"You mustn't take it personal, Mrs. Small," said Mrs. Alice comfortingly. "He's the same with all of us. You see, he's that fallen in on himself, and that feeble in his movements, that he's ashamed to have people see it, after being the fine gentleman that he was. He don't even like to have Mrs. Jones herself going in there to be with him."

"Nurses is different," said Mrs. Small firmly. "We got no time for modesty, Mrs. Alice. We scorn it. You see, we ain't exactly strangers to the 'uman body. Male and female is all the same to us, professionally speaking, of course. We look on flesh, ma'am, as you might look on a leg of mutton. Or a nice side of beef," she added as an afterthought. "Why, I can remember when Mr. Small, setting aside the aggravation of leaves, was—"

"Ssh!" said Mrs. Alice, catching sight of me again. "Little pitchers, Mrs. Small! Little pitchers!"

Mrs. Small glared at me and I retreated in a condition of bafflement. Like the mystery of the leaves, I was fated never to discover what fearful indignity Mrs. Small had perpetrated on Mr. Small when he'd been too far gone to defend himself against his wife's nursing.

At all events, I was thankful my father had been spared, for I was convinced that his extreme secrecy had nothing to do with modesty, but was somehow connected with the dreadful sounds I heard by night.

Then I wished that little pitchers had no ears at all, and I would retreat under the bedclothes so as not to hear.

The walking was much slower now, and was more of a dragging shuffle across the room. Often there were quite long pauses, during which I trembled in case the footsteps didn't start again. But they did; and the sighs would seem to drift up through the floorboards and hover in the darkness all round me, like reproachful ghosts.

Sometimes, as I lay there, I wondered if it was really my thin father who was pacing the room underneath, or whether it was some mysterious visitor who had crept in at his window, and was walking and walking, and sighing horribly, while my father looked on with bulging eyes.

But this, like everything else, remained hidden from me; and I felt that, even if I went downstairs and into my father's room, and caught that visitor in the very act of walking, he would turn and whisper:

"Ssh! Little pitchers! Little pitchers have big ears!"

My Uncle Turner had come to stay with us. He was a large, bulky man with a bullying face and a strong smell of peppermint. He was a stern, God-fearing man, and I think the feeling must have been mutual—God, I mean, being frightened of him.

He arrived one Saturday morning in a hired coach and with a great deal of baggage in order to be a support to my mother in her time of worry and trial. It was only natural, said Mrs. Alice, as my mother was his younger sister and he had always kept a soft spot for her. I don't know where he kept it but I suspect it was in a bank.

I detested him; partly because he sat at the head of the table, which, in my father's absence, I felt was my place, and partly because he never brought me a present in his life, always saying that "the boy" was well enough provided for.

He had a horrible way of greeting me by pinching my cheek between his knuckles—as if he was extracting nails—and, when the water sprang to my eyes, he would laugh loudly and declare that I was soft, which, in a boy, was apparently a very undesirable thing to be.

"Give him to me for six months, Rose," he offered my mother, "and I'll make a man of him! You won't know him, my dear!"

It was a constant nightmare of mine that, one day, I really would be sent to my Uncle Turner in order to be rendered unrecognizable to those who loved me best.

Almost the first thing he did was to take charge of Dr. Fisher, as if to show that, at last, there was somebody of importance in the house in whom the doctor might really confide.

He had long, private conversations with Dr. Fisher outside my father's room and sometimes even followed him out of the front door. Then he would pass on whatever he thought was proper for us to know, at dinner.

"I'm sorry to say that your father is a little worse, girls," he would say to my sisters; and then to me, sternly: "You must bear up, my boy. You must be a man!"

Once my father's lawyer called, and my uncle fairly pounced.

"Is everything in order? The will, I mean. Properly witnessed, eh?"

"Everything is in order, Mr. Turner. You may set your mind at rest, sir."

"Nothing unusual, eh? Nothing out of the way?"

"Really, Mr. Turner!"

At that moment, my uncle saw that I was still hanging about. He frowned and raised a finger to his lips.

"Little pitchers," I said; and went away.

That evening, my uncle was more particular than usual with his news, and he looked very solemn.

"I'm afraid, girls," he said to my sisters, "that you must prepare yourselves for the worst. Dr. Fisher has told me that your father is sinking fast."

I saw my mother reach out and hold Cissy's hand. My uncle watched glassily; then he turned to me. I think he meant to be kind; but as he believed in the need to be cruel first, we never seemed to get around to the better part of the arrangement.

"Now then! No sniveling, my boy! We must put on a good show. Nothing unmanly, eh? Really, Rose, it's a great pity you never sent him to me for six months! You wouldn't have known him! There wouldn't have been any softness, I can tell you! You must stop that childish blubbing, my boy! Stop it, I say!"

I admit that there had been tears in my eyes. But they weren't tears of sadness. I was practically crying with rage. My uncle was the most abominable man I knew.

I hadn't even been thinking about my father; or at least, not as a person. I'd been thinking of what it would be like when I sat at the head of the table.

Although the prospect of my father's death really did hang over me like a cloud, I simply couldn't help noticing that it had a substantial silver lining. I had been dreaming of coming into money and what I would do with it. In fact, at that moment, I had been wondering how much it would cost to get rid of my uncle. I was seeing myself like King Richard, beckoning a sinister figure to my side and murmuring:

"Dare you resolve to kill a friend of mine?"

After all, I thought, King Richard had disposed of his nephews, so it would be poetic justice for a nephew to dispose of his uncle.

"Straighten up, my boy!" said my uncle, banging on the table. "Don't slouch like a hunchback!"

I went to bed in a state of great anger and loneliness, and feeling that I had not a friend in the world. Even the fire in my room burned badly, as if it wished itself somewhere else.

I lay awake with nothing to look forward to but my mysterious nightly companions, the footsteps from the room below.

At last I heard the sounds of good-nights, and all the other noises of the house settling down to sleep.

The fire burned low. It had dwindled into a single bleary eye that winked at me from its jail behind the bars of the grate. Each time it vanished, there was an ashy whisper, as if the fire was clearing its throat; then it shone out again, with a sudden sharpness, as if inviting me to guess what it had been going to say.

Everything was very still, and I strained my ears to hear the creaking of my father's bed as he rose out of it for his nightly journey across the floor.

I remember lying on my side and clenching my fists as I was frightened that I'd fall asleep, or, that on this night of all nights, he wouldn't walk at all.

Then they began: the footsteps, just as before. They were very slow and halting, back and forth, back and forth, from the window to the fireplace, I judged, though I could not be sure.

Shuffle—drag . . . shuffle—drag . . . shuffle—drag . . . accompanied, as always, by the thin, drifting sighs, and the faint jingling of medicine bottles.

"A—a—ah! . . . A—a—ah! . . . A—a—ah!" as if the walker himself was reckoning up how far he'd walked, and how much further he still had to go.

Although I'd longed to hear it, now it came I found it to be the most melancholy sound in the world.

"A—a—ah! . . . A—a—ah! . . . A—"

They stopped! Suddenly, and without any warning, the sighing and the walking had come to an end.

I waited, thinking it was just a longer pause than usual. I listened fiercely and desperately for the footsteps to begin again. But there was nothing. The room underneath and its occupant stayed as quiet as the grave.

It had happened! Just as I'd always dreaded, it had happened in the middle of the night. My father was dead, and I was the only one who knew!

I sat up. The fire was out and the room was cold. I felt horribly frightened and thought of going to tell my mother. Then I remembered my Uncle Turner and thought of how he'd push everybody out of the way, and go inside my father's room, and come out looking grim and say:

"I don't want any tears or sniveling. I want you to be a man, my boy. Your father is dead."

I got out of bed. I couldn't bear the thought of his taking this last discovery on himself and shutting me out altogether. I left my room and crept downstairs in a state of panting excitement.

I reached my father's door. I stopped. I recollected that I had never seen a dead man before; and the prospect of being alone with one—and my own father into the bargain—filled me with a strong desire to be somewhere else. I pictured his dead eyes staring at me; and his freezing hand falling, suddenly and inexplicably, upon my back.

The firelight was shining under the door and streaming through the keyhole. I bent down and looked through, fully expecting another eye to be doing the same, from the other side.

I could make out only part of the window and most of the table with its loading of medicine bottles. I stood up, thinking how much better it would be to waken the household and let my mother go in first. Then my Uncle Turner came back to me, and the thought of his bullying face and shouting voice gave me courage. I've often noticed that the best in me is brought out by a strong dislike, and has nothing to do with virtue at all.

I opened the door and breathed:

"Pa!"

I'd been ready to see him lying on the floor by the window, in a quiet heap; and was prepared for it. He was not there. I looked at his bed. It was empty.

I took a very cautious step into the room, and the warm, sweetish smell of illness engulfed me. As I moved, all the medicine bottles jingled, as if they'd seen something I hadn't, and were knocking together in fright. I stopped, till *they* stopped. I could hear the rapid ticking of my father's gold watch that was on a mahogany stand by his bed. It sounded frantic and uncanny, and I remember thinking that I ought to stop it somehow.

The fire was burning brightly, and my father's chair, with its high back towards me, was drawn up close. I knew that he was sitting in it, dead.

I moved towards it. The bottles set up their frightful jingling again and the watch ticked madly, as if everything in the room, like me, was consumed with terror.

I fixed my eyes on the arms of the chair, for *his* arms; and on the feet, for *his* feet.

He was not there. The chair was empty.

I felt sick with bewilderment and dread. I knew he was somewhere in the room; but where?

I turned round. My father was standing bolt-upright behind the door. He was fully dressed, as if to go out; and he was glaring at me!

2

I DID NOT UTTER a word. The breath had not so much been knocked out of me as sucked out, in one dreadful gulp, as if the whole room had suddenly been taken short in the article of air and was getting back what it could.

I stood, holding on to the back of the chair, feeling sick with fright and guilt.

I felt frightened and guilty because my father must have known why I was there, that I'd thought he was dead and had come down to see. I felt frightened and guilty because he must have been watching me creeping about his room and looking at his gold watch.

He put out his hand and shut the door.

"What—do—you—want?" he demanded harshly.

"I—I thought I heard you, Pa," I said at length.

To my immense relief he seemed to accept this as sufficient reason for my presence, and came down a little from the gaunt height to which he'd ascended against the wall.

He was, as I've said, fully dressed; although emptily would have been nearer the mark, as his clothes hung on him in so huge and hopeless a fashion. I remember wondering if he'd actually been meaning to go outside, or whether he always dressed himself when he walked by night, as if he expected company.

"I'll go back now, Pa," I said.

He made no effort to stop me until my hand was actually on the doorknob; then he said:

"Wait, wait. What—what was it that you heard?"

"I heard you walking, Pa."

He made a most curious noise, which I can only describe as being like the ashy whisper of my fire upstairs; it was as if he'd swallowed coals and they were shifting somewhere in the bottom of his throat. He put out his hand again.

"Help me—help me to my chair."

I gave him my shoulder and he laid his hand on it; and I was astonished by how light and frail he was, like a bird. I didn't want to support him with my arm, as, to be honest, I was afraid to touch him.

We got to the chair and he sank down into it. Once more I said I'd go, and once more he said, wait, wait. I waited, while he rustled away somewhere in his chest. Then he said:

"So . . . you heard me walking?"

"Yes, Pa."

"Nothing else?"

"I—I thought I heard you sighing, Pa."

Again the ashy whisper, and he looked accusingly at the fire, as if that had done it.

"So you came down . . . to see."

I didn't answer, and waited uneasily for him to get angry. Instead, however, he only asked if I'd told my mother or anyone else? I shook my head; and he asked me if I'd ever heard him before?

I said no, because I didn't want him to think I'd been spying on him, and because I always find it easier and more natural to deny things rather than to admit them; but when he asked me again (as if he hadn't heard me the first time), I thought it best to own up.

"And you've told no one, no one at all?"

I swore I hadn't; and he lapsed into such a gloomy silence that I wondered if I'd done the wrong thing by keeping quiet.

His watch seemed to have acquired a louder tick, as if it was anxious to draw attention to some peculiarity of itself. I looked and saw that the time was one o'clock; and I remember thinking how thin the dial looked to be telling so small an hour.

"Give it to me," said my father.

"What, Pa?"

"The watch, the watch."

I fetched it and he began to fiddle with the back, and then tried to insert the key.

"Do you know how to wind a watch?" he asked. "You must give it six turns, morning and night. Never more than that. You—you must be careful. It—it cost a great deal of money."

My heart beat excitedly. Was he meaning to give it to me?

"Here, take it," he said; and when I hesitated, he added, "William," as if to show there was no mistake, that he recollected me perfectly, and even knew my name.

I took it and thanked him as warmly as I could. He smiled faintly.

"Sit down, William," he said. "Here, next to me, in front of the fire."

I sat, staring into the fire and feeling awkward as I didn't know what to say.

Nor, I think, did he. He began asking me questions about my

school and what I was learning, as if I was a stranger. Then, before I could answer, he began to talk about my mother and sisters. He said he hoped they'd always be careful about their appearance as he didn't like to think of their being shabby and careless after he was gone. I couldn't see what business this was of mine, but I nodded understandingly and said, "Yes, Pa"; and he went on again about winding up the watch at the proper times. At last he came out with:

"You're sure, William, that you've told no one about . . . about what you've heard? The—the walking . . ."

Suddenly I felt that the watch had been a reward for my silence and a bribe to continue with it. There was an overwhelming sense of secrecy and it was suffocating. Desperately I wanted to be out of that room and as far away as possible. I didn't want to hear any more about the nightly walking, as I felt there was something in it far more horrible than I'd supposed.

But it was too late. All at once my father began to jump and jerk in his chair with frightful violence, as if he was being shaken and worried by an enormous invisible dog. He clapped his hand to his mouth and his eyes were dreadful; then, when it was over and he was quiet again, he took his hand away, and I noticed that he kept it tightly clenched, as if there was money in it.

I wanted to run and get my mother; but he wouldn't let me leave him. I asked if I could get him some medicine; but he didn't want that, either. I didn't know what to do, so I held on to his hand—not the clenched one, which he hid from me, but the other that was clasping the arm of the chair.

He began to talk, or, rather, to whisper, and it was like dead leaves. At first I thought he was delirious, because it was all about foxes being caught. Then I understood that he hadn't meant the animals, but a place—a place called "Foxes Court," which was near Holborn, in London. Also he mentioned somebody called "K'Nee," several times, always pronouncing the K as if it was a cough.

"But it was all a—a long time ago," he mumbled, shaking his head as if to rid himself of the memory. "Before you were born . . . nothing to do with you. Before your mother . . . nothing to do with her. Before—before everything . . ."

He stopped, and I thought he was going to jump and jerk again, as his eyes had got the same dreadful look. But it was something else.

He had begun to whisper about a man called "Diamond, Alfred Diamond." Over and over again, he kept saying, "Diamond . . . Diamond . . . Diamond!" until I hated that Mr. Diamond with all my heart; for I could see the grief and misery his very recollection caused.

Suddenly he turned over the hand I'd been holding, and gripped my wrist as hard as he could.

"Mr. Diamond was my friend and partner," he said. "He trusted me and I cheated him. If Alfred Diamond is dead, I killed him. If he is alive, it is only to curse me with every breath he draws. Now, *now* you know why I walk and sigh, walk and sigh . . . Your father, my son, is nothing but a scoundrel and a thief."

He didn't say any more. He sat, staring into the fire as if he was quite alone. He had let go of my hand and I wondered if that meant I could go back to bed.

I had an odd feeling that he wanted me to say something, perhaps even to comfort him; but I couldn't. I got up.

"Good night, Pa," I said.

He lifted his head.

"Good night, William."

There was an anxious, almost pleading look on his face, as if, now he had told me his secret, he hoped everything was all right. He looked sunk and feeble; and nothing like my father at all.

I left the room and went back upstairs. As I was about to get into bed, I saw that I still had the watch. I wanted to throw it out of the window, or to stamp it into fragments. I hated it; and I hated my father, too.

I felt utterly deceived. My father had cheated me just as he had cheated Mr. Diamond. My father, that stern and upright man, whose praise I'd longed for, and for whose friendship I would have given the world, was nothing but a swindler and a thief!

I put the watch on my chest of drawers, meaning to give it back in the morning. I got into bed; and then I heard him begin to walk again. I tried to shut out the noise, but the footsteps seemed to be right inside my head. Back and forth, back and forth he dragged, as his crime continued to haunt him—and me!—though he walked ten thousand miles.

If only, I thought, he'd been dead when I'd first gone down! *Then*, the secret would have stayed a secret, and been well worth the keeping.

When I woke up, the sun was shining and a good deal of my anger was gone. I hadn't changed my mind; I still meant to return the watch; but I had decided to tell my father that I had forgiven him, that it was all right, and there was no further need for him to walk by night.

I dressed, put the watch in my pocket and went downstairs. My uncle met me in the hall.

"You are not to go to school today," he said.

He clasped his hands behind his back as if to restrain his natural desire to pinch my cheek and make me cry.

"Now, no sniveling, my boy. I want you to be a man. I am sorry to have to tell you that your father is dead."

3

THE DAYS IMMEDIATELY AFTER my father's death were very strange, like a solemn holiday—a kind of Black Christmas. Candles were kept burning in broad day, and the curtains drawn, so that the winter sunshine strained at every window and made the rooms rickety with bright chinks and slits, as if the house was leaking darkness at every joint.

My mother and my sisters seemed to have come out in black so suddenly that it was as if they'd been caught in a shower of soot; and a black ribbon was tied round my sleeve to mark me out as an object of especial tenderness and concern.

My mother repeatedly embraced me and said tearfully that she hoped I would be a good, kind boy; and Cissy, my older sister, told me that I was now *Mr.* Jones and that, when the time came, it would be my duty to give her away in marriage. Rebecca, the other one, who was excessively virtuous and plain, came up to my room and sat on the bed and cried officiously; and even my uncle went about as if his feet hurt.

It was, in an odd way, quite a cheerful time, as there were always visitors sitting in the best parlor and drinking Madeira wine.

Dr. Fisher came once; but after that it was the parson who took his place and always called me "young man" and put his hand on my shoulder as if he was going to hit me and was steadying me while he took aim.

"Now that your dear father has been taken from us, young man," he would begin; regardless of the fact that my father had not yet been taken anywhere, but was still in his room and with a strong smell of vinegar and aromatic herbs.

I had not been allowed to see him until after the undertaker's people had been and put him in his coffin.

I tried to find out, from Mrs. Alice, who'd found him that morning, whether he'd been sitting in his chair, or lying on the floor, or back in his bed. I wanted to know if he'd got undressed again after I'd left him.

I still thought that he'd been meaning to go outside, and, from what he'd told me, to go to Foxes Court and find Mr. Diamond. I wanted very much to think that he'd given up that idea and, after my visit, had decided to die in peace. I regretted bitterly that I hadn't said more to him in the way of comfort, and Mrs. Alice's warnings of waking up one morning and finding it was too late haunted me badly.

"Was he in his bed, Mrs. Alice?"

"Never you mind," said she; and poured me out a glass of raisin wine, and said I was a poor, fatherless boy, and began to cry, which made her look more like an ancient baby than ever.

It wasn't until later that I discovered why my father had been fully dressed; and that the journey he'd been proposing to make was a good deal further than London and Foxes Court.

I overheard my uncle talking about it to the parson on the day before the funeral. Although it was the law that you had to be buried in a woolen shroud on account of helping the wool trade, my father had hated the idea of it and insisted that he was to be laid to rest in his best clothes. It was his last solemn vanity, even if he was fined for it.

When I heard this, and understood, I felt cold with dread. My father must have known he was going to die that night; and had made himself ready. He'd known that he'd never see me again, and that the words he spoke to me would be his last. Consequently those words now became immensely important; and the scene between my father and me burned in my mind as if it would never go out.

The funeral marked the last day of the weird holiday, and the ending of the daytime candlelight. I wore undertakers' gloves and a huge black weeper round my hat, that kept blowing out in the wind by the graveside, like a pirate's flag.

My mother's family from St. Albans came down in three carriages, and there was an old lady with a mannish face, who was supposed to be a distant relation of my father's, and the only one he had. When the St. Albans people went away, they must have taken the old lady with them, by mistake, I supposed, as I never saw her again.

I wondered if Foxes Court had heard about the funeral, and I looked round the church for people who might have come from my father's old life. But there were only neighbors and people from Hertford who I knew.

I remember, afterwards, how pitifully empty the house seemed; and my father's room, with its door left open, his bed as smooth as marble, and all the medicine bottles gone, made me feel, for the first time, that *he* had really gone, and would never, never come back.

My uncle told me, quite gently for him, to bear up and be a man, and that my father would not have been pleased to see me blubbering like a girl.

We were at dinner: a late, sad, leftover meal. I had been staring mistily at the leg of mutton Mrs. Alice had put on the table, and remembering Mrs. Small, the nurse, to whom human beings, male and female, had meant no more than butcher's meat might have meant to Mrs. Alice; and I'd been wondering if Mrs. Alice had been feeling the same, only the other way round, of course.

My uncle spoke to my mother.

"Have you asked her yet, Rose?"

"No. Not yet. I—I thought I'd leave it till tomorrow."

"I think you must ask her tonight, Rose. After all, it's a valuable object and quite a temptation."

"I can't believe that she took it!"

"Perhaps she put it in a drawer and forgot to tell you? You mustn't neglect it, Rose. If she's been dishonest, she must be made to admit it."

I realized they were talking about my father's gold watch. My uncle had noticed that the mahogany stand was empty and suspected that Mrs. Alice, or one of the maids, had stolen the watch.

It was in my waistcoat pocket. I could hear it ticking away like an enormous insect. I felt my face grow very red. I knew I ought to have got up and said, loudly and truthfully, "I've got my father's watch. He gave it to me before he died." But somehow I felt unequal to it. Instead, I put my hand over my ticking pocket and hoped nobody would hear it.

"What's that, my boy?" said my uncle sharply. "What have you got there?"

He never missed anything, and must have seen my change of color. I felt quite ill as I knew there was no hope. If I didn't own up he'd search me and that would make matters worse.

"It's the watch," I mumbled. "It—it's Pa's watch."

My mother looked relieved; but my sister Rebecca immediately said that I had no right to it, and that it was perfectly disgusting.

"But Pa gave it to me!" I shouted angrily.

My mother, trying to keep the peace, said to my uncle:

"There! You see? It's all right. Nobody stole it. William has it . . . and, I suppose, it really ought to be his."

Rebecca began to complain; but my uncle told her to keep quiet and said to my mother:

"I think you'd better leave this to me, Rose."

There was an awful, anticipatory note in his voice, like a hangman about to enjoy his trade. He turned to me.

"Now, my boy, show me that watch."

I held it up and then put it back in my pocket as quickly as I could, as if I was performing a conjuring trick with it. My uncle nodded.

"Yes. You told the truth. You have the watch. Now I want you to be very careful before you answer again. How did you get the watch, my boy?"

"I told her—Rebecca! Pa gave it to me!"

"And when did he give it to you?"

"The night—the night he died!"

Immediately I saw my uncle give a triumphant smile as he thought he'd caught me out.

"That's not true, my boy. I was in the room when you said good night to your father. He never gave you anything. Come now—admit it, admit it!"

"It wasn't then! It was much later . . . in—in the middle of the night! I heard him . . . and—and went down to see! That's when he gave it to me!"

My uncle looked incredulous.

"You heard your sick father in the middle of the night and never called your mother or me? Now that's a lie, my boy. That's a wicked, wicked lie!"

I protested that it wasn't, it wasn't, and offered, in proof of my veracity, the fact that my father had even told me about winding the watch up, six turns every morning and night.

Even as I said it, I knew it sounded feeble and lame, and I saw my sister Rebecca staring at me contemptuously, as if she could have invented a much better tale. But I was in a frightful situation. It was absolutely impossible for me to explain that I hadn't called for help because I detested my uncle so much!

My uncle lost his temper altogether. He began banging on the table as if it was my head, and he was determined to crack it, like a nut, and get at what was inside.

"Now see what comes of indulging him, Rose!" he bellowed. "Now you can see how he's turned out! If only you'd let me have him for that six months when I begged you, none of this would have happened! Now he's become a liar and a thief! Look at him! A boy well provided for, with everything to look forward to! And what does he do? He steals from his dead father—from your husband, Rose! He can't even wait for his father to be cold in his grave! And what a father! A fine, upright man who never did an underhand thing in his life! We can only be thankful that he isn't here to see it! That such a father should have such a son!"

I know I should have kept quiet and let the storm blow over. I know it would have been more sensible to have shrugged my shoulders and said that my uncle was entitled to his opinion but that it was not necessarily the right one; but I was, after all, only twelve years old, the youngest at the table and very frightened and distressed; and the awful banging on the table only made matters worse, so that I felt that, if I didn't shout and scream back, my head really would split open and everything would come out.

All I wanted was to defend myself against that large, violent man, and to make him believe me.

So, with this in mind, I told him, at the top of my voice, that he was the liar, not me. I told him that he didn't know anything about my father at all; and, in order to substantiate my claim, I banged on the table as he did, only with both fists, and shouted that my father was not an upright man, but was a swindler and a cheat and had told me so himself! I shrieked out all about Mr. Diamond and Foxes Court, and, for good measure, swore that all the money we'd come into was on account of a mean and treacherous crime!

I suppose I must have presented quite an extraordinary sight, shrieking and banging on the table and blackening my dead father's name. But I never thought of it like that.

It was only when I noticed that my mother and my sisters were staring at me in horror that I realized what I'd done. I think even my uncle was taken aback to discover that I'd turned out to be even worse than he'd supposed.

"That will be enough," he said quietly, when I finished up in tears of misery and indignation. "That will be quite enough, my boy. Go to your room. Your mother and I will decide what is to be done with you."

He didn't even tell me to stop sniveling and be a man. He looked at me in the most extraordinary way; and, for a moment, I thought I'd actually frightened him. But if I had, it wasn't half so much as he'd frightened me.

I went upstairs shaking with terror as to what fate would be decided for me. The threatened six months would be at least a year; and I had some thoughts of hanging myself with a note attached, to the effect that I hoped everybody would be sorry for what they'd done.

I lay on my bed without getting undressed and tried to hear what was being said downstairs; but they all kept their voices down. I wondered if Cissy, or Mrs. Alice, would come up to see me and tell me not to worry too much. But no one came. Then I remembered that I hadn't wound up the watch.

I went to kneel by the fire so that I could see to put the key in. The time was half-past eleven.

The day had been a long one. The funeral might have taken place last year, and all the departed guests no more than solemn figures in a dream. I would not have been surprised if the open grave I'd stood by that morning was already grassed over and half forgotten. I wondered what my father was thinking as he lay in the darkness under the ground.

I wondered if he knew about the frantic unhappiness he had brought about by giving me his watch? I wondered if he knew that he had left me unutterably alone?

I remember I cried a good deal and confided, to the burning coals, that I wanted my father to come back and save me, by telling everybody that I had told the truth. But I knew, in my heart of hearts, that, even if I cried myself bone-dry, he would never come back and that I must shift for myself.

Then I knew that I would have to find Mr. Diamond, and make him come back and confess that my father had cheated him, and that I had told the truth.

"Mr. Diamond . . ." I murmured, as if the name was a talisman. "Foxes Court . . . Mr. K'Nee . . ."

Suddenly it all seemed very simple, and I wondered that I hadn't thought of it before; and I drifted into an agreeable dream of producing Mr. Diamond at the dining table, with a burst of music and a shout of triumph.

I must have fallen asleep. All at once, it seemed, the house was quiet, the fire was low, and I saw that it was one o'clock. I was still lying on the floor, with my head resting against the fender and a general stiffness all over.

For a moment, I remembered having had a good idea, and felt quite pleased . . . until I remembered what it had been. That I should go and find Mr. Diamond and bring him back home.

It was hopeless. Even if Mr. Diamond still lived, how could I ever find him? How could I even leave the house without my uncle seizing me and dragging me back? And supposing I did get out of the house, where would I go? To Foxes Court? How would I find it in a huge place like London; and who would take any notice of a boy of twelve? I would be robbed, murdered, and thrown into the River Thames.

These and a hundred other heavy considerations weighed me down and plunged me into such a gloom that I cursed the wretched watch over and over again.

"Why, why did you give it to me?" I demanded of the dying fire. "Why did you tell me everything when you knew you were going to die? Why . . . why?"

The fire whispered harshly and threw up a brief flame. I stood up, meaning to go to bed. I felt very cold, and I remember thinking that the weather must have taken a turn for the worse, as if, like me, it had decided there was no hope and was appalled.

I stood, holding the ticking watch in my hand, and shivering. Then, as if somehow I'd expected it all the time, I heard the most terrible sound.

I swear that this is true. I heard, quite distinctly, from the empty room underneath, the sound of my dead father's footsteps, dragging across the floor!

He had left his coffin and come back! He was down there, walking back and forth, back and forth, and sighing ceaselessly over the wrong he had done and never put right.

Then I knew that, until I found Mr. Diamond, neither my father nor I would ever have peace. Night after night he would shuffle and drag across the floor, and night after night I would hear him; unless I left the house and set out on the journey that would lay his ghost.

4

TO LEAVE A HOUSE where you have lived all your life, where your best possessions are scattered in every room from attic to cellar, is no easy matter; but to do so in secrecy, in the middle of the night, with no candle, and fearful that every creaking floorboard is betraying you and every ill-fitting cupboard and drawer—no matter how carefully you open it—is shrieking aloud: "He's running away! He's running away!" is an undertaking to stop the heart and freeze the blood in your veins.

I had a silver tankard; but it was in the kitchen, so I had to leave it behind; I had a folding fruit-knife with a mother-of-pearl handle; but it was in the dining room, so I had to leave that, too.

Fortunately my money was in a purse in my own room. I had seven guineas given to me on birthdays by my grandmother in St. Albans. She was my Uncle Turner's mother; but you would never have known it.

Remembering my father's dislike of shabbiness, and fearing that Mr. Diamond would turn out to be the same, I put on my best clothes and took a change of linen; or, rather, a sameness of linen twice over, as I wore two shirts. Also I tied two pairs of stockings round my neck, as if I was being strangled by legs.

I took these precautions rather than carry a bundle, which, I feared, would have advertised me too openly as a runaway. I thought about leaving a note, but decided against it as it might have been found too soon and I'd have been hauled back and locked up, probably for the rest of my life.

I left my house at half-past five. It was still pitch-black outside, and very quiet; but that didn't stop me seeing my uncle behind every tree and stepping out to confront me, like a monster, at every turn in the narrow winding road.

I got to Hertford an hour before the coaching office opened, and spent the time pressed into doorways and hiding behind posts as I was convinced that every passerby knew all about me and was going directly to my uncle to inform him that his scoundrelly nephew was running away.

At last the coach office opened and I bought a place on the London coach from a clerk who, I feared, had only pretended to go and get change and was, in reality, galloping like mad back to my house with the news of my flight.

Even when I was actually sitting in the coach and on my way, and Hertford was behind me, I was not easy in my mind. I stared cautiously at my dozing fellow passengers and became convinced that they were united in a conspiracy to lull me into a false sense of security and were silently preparing to have me seized at the very first stop. When one of them got out, I thought he'd gone for a constable; and when another got in, I thought he *was* a constable.

It was only when we got to Waltham Cross, and changed horses, and ate breakfast, that I was able to put my Uncle Turner behind me and to think about the great city that was only another hour and a half away.

Although I had never been to London, I had heard a great deal about it, chiefly from Mrs. Alice, who had been there when she was a girl. It must have been a long time ago, as I had a picture of the town consisting entirely of St. Paul's Cathedral and the Tower, which was always kept smart with traitors' heads.

Mrs. Alice had once seen the Lord Mayor, but she could find no words to describe his magnificence; and she had been taken to see a highwayman hanged at Tyburn, where they sold the best pies in the world.

All in all, I was prepared for a place of dazzling splendor and excitement that would burst out upon the road ahead like a gorgeous thunderclap. I wouldn't have been surprised if great golden gates had swung open and trumpeters had sounded our arrival from the walls.

Instead of which, at half-past eleven, we came to a dismal huddle of broken houses loitering round an oversized church, and a few market gardens that seemed to be growing nothing more than bricks. Then we went over cobbles and turned into a dirty inn-yard. We stopped and everybody got out. I never saw such a miserable place in all my life.

"Is this—is *this* London?" I asked an ostler, half expecting to be laughed at for making such a mistake.

He gazed at me pityingly, as if he understood that it was all too much for me. Then he nodded.

"This is Lunnon, all right!" he said, with every appearance of affection and pride. "Best town in the world!"

I looked up. The sky, which, in Hertford, had been of a clear, wintry blue, was now yellow, as if it was much older and none too well. Even the sun had a bloodshot look and seemed to be in danger of going out.

"Lovely day," said the ostler. "Nothin' like Lunnon in the sunshine!"

Somewhat depressed, I asked him if he knew a place called Foxes Court?

He scratched his head and couldn't say that he did.

"It's near a place called Holborn," I said.

"Ah!" said he, brightening up and pointing knowledgeably straight at a brick wall. "You wanna go dahn that way, sec'nd on yer left, then 'long Bishopsgit, right turn and 'long past Bedlam 'orspittle, left at Aldersgit, right at Newgit, an' yc're practickly there! Can't miss it! 'Bout a hour, I should say."

I hadn't understood a word he'd said; but I thanked him and set off, meaning to ask again as soon as he was out of sight.

I walked and walked and the town began to close in upon me, not with splendor, but with gray, stony, twisted limbs, that were endless roads and lanes and streets.

There was a strange smell in the air, that grew stronger and stronger. It was something of cheese, something of cabbage, something of boiled meat, and a good deal of sulphur; so that I felt I was in that part of hell where they did the cooking.

There were other signs of hell, too . . . such as a gigantic uproar composed of grinding iron wheels, scraping shovels, squealing horses and the never-ending shouts and curses of demons and damned as they got in each other's way.

Everybody was angry. There was anger in the very air. When I asked the way, I was answered angrily, or not at all. A man pulled me out of the way of a cart, and asked me angrily if I wanted to be killed? Angrily I answered, no, and was I anywhere near Holborn yet?

He told me to keep a civil tongue in my head and sent me off down a great street where all the world seemed to be rushing along one way, as if the street had been tipped and they were all swirling down into a drain.

I never saw so many people before; and, I thought, so many people had never seen me. In Hertford, and on the coach, I'd been frightened that everybody knew me and knew what I was doing. Here I was even more frightened because nobody knew me and nobody cared what I was doing.

The town was huge beyond belief; it was a hundred towns all jumbled up together; it was a sprawling calamity of brick, stone, and noise through which I was doomed to walk and walk until I died, asking for:

"Holborn . . . Holborn . . . Can you please tell me the way to Holborn, sir?"

"Holborn? Are you blind, lad? You're right in the middle of it! This is Holborn!"

I ran after the gentleman, thanking him with all my heart. I couldn't believe my good fortune . . . until I began to ask for Foxes Court. Nobody knew it. Some thought it this way, some that, and some thought it might be over yonder, on the other side of the river. But at last somebody did know it.

He knew it like the back of his hand, he said; and held that object up, and I could see that it was such a tangle of gnarled veins that it might well have been a map of that part of the town, colored in to show the dirt.

He directed me down a narrow passage between two buildings, with the advice that I should follow my nose, as if I was a hound, and foxes still lived in Foxes Court, and I would infallibly sniff it out.

As I walked along the passage, which was dark and seemed to have a running cold in its bricks, the noise of the town receded and what at first I took to be another noise, crept cautiously into its place. This other noise grew more and more pervasive until eventually it had blotted out the last faint sounds of the town.

With a shock I realized that this noise was silence. The passage had ended; and there before me was a secret patch of grass, a secret tree, and a secret rectangle of houses that seemed to have been trapped, forgotten and died. It was Foxes Court.

Afterwards I discovered that there were many such quiet enclosures in the town—little pockets lined with green, in which it kept small, tattered mementos of the countryside where it had been born.

But as I stood and gazed at the stones over which my father must have walked, and the rusty seat that encircled the tree where once he must have sat, and the tall thin houses among which he must have moved with easy familiarity, I felt it to be the most deeply concealed and haunted place in all the world.

5

MR. K'NEE (ATTORNEY-AT-LAW) LIVED on the third floor of the darkest and dirtiest house in the court.

According to a signboard nailed inside the doorway, he shared the premises with an astonishing number of other Attorneys, Solicitors and Notaries, all of whom were ready to Draw Up Wills, Convey Property, and Administer the Swearing of Oaths; which, at that time, I supposed to mean that they offered facilities for gentlemen to come and curse in private, rather than out in the open street.

If so, then some of them must have been in too much of a hurry to wait; for they'd scrawled their curses all over the walls. I wondered if any of them had been Mr. Diamond's, when he'd found out that he'd been cheated by his friend. I began to mount the stairs.

"Where do you think you're going?"

I stopped and came down again.

The voice came from a newspaper with two hands and two feet, sitting on a chair half in a cupboard under the stairs.

"If you please," I said, "I'm going to see Mr. K'Nee."

The newspaper shifted slightly, and a large, queerly refined face appeared round the edge of it. I was examined.

"If it's a Document," said the face, "you can give it to me. If it's a Summons, you can hand it in yourself."

The face vanished.

"It—it's private," I said.

"Got an appointment?"

"No . . . no."

"Won't see you, then. Good day."

"But I must see him! I must—I must!"

With a sound of irritation the newspaper was put aside and the owner of the refined face got up off his chair. For a moment, I thought he'd stepped into a hole, as he seemed to go down at least six inches; then I saw that he was a dwarf.

"Must? Must?" he said angrily. "Must is for the king! Come along then. I'll take you up, your majesty!"

He stumped fiercely across the hall, unlocked a door and stepped inside a tall wooden box, rather like a large coffin. It turned out to be a kind of hoist, operated by two ropes on which the dwarf pulled vigorously, and, I thought, with pleasure.

It was the strangest of journeys, rising up secretly through the filthy, rickety old house, where lawyers lived like mice, and Mr. K'Nee waited for the son of Mr. Jones.

At last we stopped and I stepped out on the third floor landing, which differed only from the others by being a little dirtier.

"Pay me when you go out," said the dwarf, and sank away, leaving a terrible hole behind.

I knocked on Mr. K'Nee's door and was told to come in; and Mr. K'Nee's clerk, a smart young man in very cramped quarters, changed what had been a smile into a frown when he saw that it was only a boy.

"If you please, sir," I said. "I would like to see Mr. K'Nee."

"So would a lot of people," said he, sitting back in his chair and tilting it against the wall, which was only a couple of inches off. "So would a lot of people, young feller-me-lad. That's why we 'ave clerks and appointments. Mr. K'Nee's time is valuable. We can't 'ave 'im wastin' it on boys from the street."

"Please, please, sir—I must see Mr. K'Nee! I've come a long way . . ."

At this point, I'm sorry to say, I began to cry. It seemed intolerable that, after all I'd suffered, I should be turned away.

"Who's that, Jenkins?" came a voice from the other side of the inner door.

"Just a boy, Mr. K'Nee. I'll send 'im packin' in a minute."

"What does he want?"

"To see you, Mr. K'Nee."

"What's his name?"

"What's your name, boy?" asked Jenkins severely.

"William Jones, sir."

"William Jones, Mr. K'Nee."

"Don't know him. Send him away."

"Jones! Jones!" I shouted desperately. "I'm William Jones—the son of Mr. David Jones who's just died! Please, Mr. K'Nee!"

There was a pause in which Jenkins busied himself with a paper and pretended not to be interested.

"David Jones?" came Mr. K'Nee's voice. "David Jones in coffee?"

"Yes! Yes!"

The door opened.

"Come inside, David Jones's son! Come inside!"

Mr. K'Nee was not alone. There was a Mr. Needleman with him and they'd been playing cards.

Mr. K'Nee was an old man with a face like a clenched fist from which a great nose stuck out like a shiny prominent knuckle. It was a clever, ugly face; and I thought he was a clever, ugly man.

I didn't see much of Mr. Needleman as he was standing up. Here I must explain that there seemed to be no window in Mr. K'Nee's room and the only light came from three or four deeply shaded candles and a quiet fire. Consequently the upper part of the room was cast in heavy shadow; and when people sat down, you couldn't see much more than mouths, chins and hands.

Mr. Needleman, as I've said, was standing up, and he might as well have had a black bag over his head.

"I always thought," said Mr. Needleman, when Mr. K'Nee had shut the door, opened it sharply as if to see if Jenkins's ear was to it, and shut it again, "that David Jones was a smart man."

"So he was," agreed Mr. K'Nee, sitting down at his desk. "Very smart."

"Then the boy here don't take after him. Shabby little ruffian with stockings tied round his neck."

"That's very sharp of you, Mr. Needleman," said Mr. K'Nee. "Quite up to your name." And he made a little movement with his finger suggestive of a needle going through something soft, like me.

His gesture really did seem to puncture me, and let a large part of my confidence escape. I felt that Mr. K'Nee did not even believe that I was David Jones's son. I felt lost and alone as I realized that, to these two gentlemen, I was nothing more than a travel-stained ruffian, come in off the street.

Mr. Needleman sat down beside Mr. K'Nee, and came into view as far as the bottom of his nose.

For a moment I thought of throwing myself on their mercy; but somehow I felt that that article would turn out to be uncomfortable, and that I'd be impaled on it, like a spike. Then I remembered the watch. I produced it and Mr. K'Nee examined it carefully, passed it to Mr. Needleman, and then gave it back.

"Yes," he said. "This is David Jones's watch all right."

At once I felt such a rush of happiness and affection towards Mr. K'Nee for believing that I was my father's son, that my chief purpose seemed to have been achieved. I almost forgot about Mr. Diamond.

"So," said Mr. K'Nee to Mr. Needleman. "David Jones isn't with us any more. He was a younger man than me. It comes to us all, Needleman; it comes to us all. Has he been gone long, David Jones's son? Passed away, I mean?"

"A week, sir. He was buried yesterday morning."

"Leaves a widow, I suppose?"

"Yes, sir. And I've got two sisters—"

"Well provided for?"

"Oh yes! We've a big house in—"

"—Don't tell where!" said Mr. K'Nee, abruptly cutting me off.

"I don't want to know where David Jones hid himself, living or dead."

As he said that, I saw Mr. Needleman look at him sharply. In fact, Mr. Needleman, as if flattered by Mr. K'Nee's observation about the aptness of his name, kept on making sharp, sudden movements all the time.

"Well," said Mr. K'Nee. "You have your father's watch. What else have you got of your father's, that brings you to Foxes Court?"

At once I felt unaccountably guilty, as if Mr. K'Nee, like my uncle, suspected me of being a thief.

"Nothing nothing! That's all he gave me . . . just before he died!"

"So why have you run away from your comfortable home and come to see Mr. K'Nee in Foxes Court?"

"I—I haven't run away . . ."

"Come come! David Jones's son doesn't burst in, like a mad thing, with stockings round his neck, and wearing two shirts, just to pass the time of day! Why have you come?"

"I—I want to find Mr. Diamond, sir!"

Another sharp movement from Mr. Needleman.

"What for?" This from Mr. K'Nee, who seemed to respond to Mr. Needleman's sharp movements as if he was being invisibly pricked. I felt that Mr. K'Nee without Mr. Needleman, would have been a different man altogether.

"I—I wanted to tell him that—that Pa was dead," I said. Although I guessed that Mr. K'Nee knew all about my father having ruined Mr. Diamond, I felt I couldn't say anything about it. In fact, I found it hard to say anything—even to breathe, at times— in that close, secretive room with its hovering shadow, like a large black hat, pulled down over Mr. Needleman's and Mr. K'Nee's eyes.

Mr. Needleman had picked up the cards he'd been playing with, and studied them intently. Mr. K'Nee asked me if my father had had a long illness and if he'd talked much about the old days in London and Foxes Court.

I told him that it had been a long illness, but my father had only mentioned himself and Foxes Court on the last night of all, and to me alone. I kept the ghostly footsteps out of it; which, I suppose, made him think that I was hiding something of value.

"So why don't you ask him?" said Mr. Needleman, snapping up the cards he'd been holding spread out in a fan.

"Do you think he knows anything?" murmured Mr. K'Nee.

"So why is he here, asking for Diamond?"

"He's only a child."

"So he's a child. But a man like David Jones don't go to his grave with ten thousand pounds in a drawer and never say a word. That's not in human nature."

Mr. K'Nee picked up his own cards and, holding them close to his waistcoat, examined them one by one.

"Do you know what we've been talking about, David Jones's son?"

I confessed that I didn't, and that the conversation had been mysterious in the extreme.

So Mr. K'Nee told me about a curious and tantalizing circumstance that had long fascinated Foxes Court. There was a story that my father had accomplished a stroke of business before he'd retired and that ten thousand pounds, either in banknotes, gold or diamonds—the matter was in dispute—had vanished into thin air.

Nobody knew what had become of it; and no trace of it had ever been found. Mr. Needleman, in spite of Mr. K'Nee's shaking his head, was convinced that my father had deposited it in some place of safety in the town. He was sure it was still waiting to be found. He kept urging Mr. K'Nee, with sharp movements of his head and elbow, to ask me, over and over again, if my father had given me anything else besides his watch. Had he mentioned any particular place, any particular name, had he given me a key, perhaps, or a piece of paper with an address?

As the questioning went on, I felt that Mr. Needleman and Mr. K'Nee were like two masked old pirates, digging in a dark place for long-buried treasure; and that I was becoming infected with the same fantastic hope of finding it, intact and undisturbed, after twenty years. I went over and over in my mind, every word my father had uttered on that night before he'd died; but I could find nothing of any help.

At length, Mr. K'Nee—but not, I thought, Mr. Needleman— gave up.

"You had better go back to your home, David Jones's son," he said. "Wherever it may be."

"It's in—" I began; when once again he stopped me.

"Come here, David Jones's son," he said, beckoning me to his side. "Now Mr. Needleman and I are playing cards. These are mine. You notice that I keep them hidden from him. If I didn't, I might lose. As it is, he doesn't know what I hold. So . . . he plays a Queen . . . and I trump it! He plays a King . . . and I trump it! He plays an Ace, even . . . and I trump that, too! Always something in reserve, David Jones's son. Always something kept back in reserve."

I thanked him for his advice.

"Goodbye, David Jones's son. My regards to the widow and the daughters."

"But what about Mr. Diamond!" I cried. "I wanted to see Mr. Diamond!"

Another sharp movement from Mr. Needleman.

"Forget about Mr. Diamond," said Mr. K'Nee. "Go back to your comfortable home. This is no place for you. You don't hold the right cards, David Jones's son; and even if you did, you wouldn't know how to play them. Go back before someone thinks you hold the Ace of Trumps, and knocks you on the head."

"But I must find Mr. Diamond first! I must!"

"Mr. Diamond," said Mr. K'Nee harshly, "Mr. Alfred Diamond is dead."

For a moment I did not take in what he said. I stood there, looking so utterly bewildered that Mr. K'Nee repeated his words.

"Mr. Diamond is dead."

I felt such a tremendous rush of dismay that I could scarcely stand up. The strange, half-black room, with its secret mouths and chins and grasping hands, began to swim in a mist of misery as I realized what I had done. I had fled from my home with only one object, only one hope in the world. Now, at a single blow, I had lost both: my hope, and my home. I dared not go back; and I could not go on.

The two attorneys sat at their cards, and made no effort to help me out of the room.

I tried to look nonchalant when I got into the outer office, as if I'd concluded a successful piece of business and was quite calm.

Jenkins, the smart young clerk, however, was not deceived.

"Cheer up, David Jones's son!" he muttered, assisting me to the outer door. "It ain't the end of the world. Guess what? You ain't the only son. Mr. Diamond's got one, too. 'Live and kickin'.' Meet me in the Horse Boy, back of Mallerd's Court at eight o'clock on the nail; and I'll—"

Mr. K'Nee's door opened and Jenkins shut up as if he'd been slammed.

"Remember what I told you, David Jones's son," said Mr. K'Nee; "about the Ace of Trumps."

6

REJECTING MY FIRST IDEA, which had been to throw myself down the black hole into which the dwarf had earlier vanished, I went down by the stairs instead.

The sudden news of Mr. Diamond's death had put me into such a frantic state of mind that I found myself, without thinking, stopping on every landing and reading aloud the scrawled-up curses that seemed to cover every single wall in that hateful house.

I wondered how many people, like me, had come out of the various dusty doors and thought of jumping down the hole in despair; and then, like me, had changed their minds because of some crumb of hope a lawyer or his clerk had let fall, and so contented themselves with merely cursing the world instead of leaving it.

I wondered how many people had come out of the doors without any hope, and thrown themselves down; and how did the dwarf ever get their broken bodies off the top of his hoist? I wondered if that was how Mr. Diamond had died, and if it had been just after he'd found out that my father had swindled him?

"If Alfred Diamond is dead, I killed him," my father had said.

As I remembered his exact words, I remembered the mystery of the ten thousand pounds, and Mr. Needleman's curious insistence that I might have been told something of great importance; and I had an uncomfortable feeling that Mr. K'Nee's remark, about the Ace of Trumps and being knocked on the head for it, had not been entirely idle. I wondered what it was that I knew that could be of danger to me.

"Oh no you don't!" came a voice from behind the stairs. "Oh no you don't creep off without paying!"

It was the dwarf. He emerged from his cupboard and hobbled towards me with his hand outstretched. I saw that his fingers were so short that they might have been chopped off.

"That'll be a penny," he said.

I gave it to him. He stood on tiptoe and looked into my purse, as if to make sure I could afford it.

"Why didn't you shout for me to fetch you down? That's what I'm here for."

"I—I didn't think of it."

"There's notices up. Call for Mr. Seed."

"I didn't see them."

"Too busy reading rude words, eh? I heard you. You ought to have read the notice and called."

He was a very angry little man and had taken great offense over not being called. I supposed it was because he'd have earned another penny by taking me down in his hoist; so I offered him one.

IIe took it—or, rather, snatched it—and at the same time snapped that he wasn't a child to be bought off so cheap. He was, he judged—turning his great face sideways and estimating me—about four times my age and forty times as clever.

I wondered if I ought to offer him a third penny to placate him, as I wanted to ask him the way to the Horse Boy, where I was to meet Mr. K'Nee's clerk. But I hesitated as he seemed unpleasantly sensitive and ready to fly into a rage at anything.

I felt he was sneering at me for being better dressed than he was, and having more money, and being taller, even though he was four times as old and forty times as clever.

"Well?"

"Please could you tell me," I began; when a voice from upstairs shouted:

"Seed! Mr. Seed, please! Second floor!"

"Wait here!" said the dwarf; and hobbled away into his hoist and shut the door after him.

I waited, listening to the shuddering of the hoist ascending, and then coming down. The door opened and there was the dwarf, with a full-grown gentleman beside him, exactly as if he'd made him up out of nothing, inside the wooden box. I thought the dwarf looked rather pleased with himself. The gentleman paid him and went away.

"Well," said the dwarf. "Please could I tell you what?"

"The way to the Horse Boy," I said. "At the back of Mallerd's Court."

"I could," said the dwarf. "But it won't do you any good."

"Why not?" I asked, wondering if, somehow, the dwarf knew all about Mr. Diamond's son, and knew that my errand would be hopeless. Indeed, at that time, anything seemed possible in that house of lawyers and curses all hiding from the light.

"Why not? Why not?" muttered the dwarf, stumping irritably on his short legs to the front door. "The boy asks me why not. That's why not!" He opened the door; and I saw beyond it, what appeared to be another, composed of yellowish gray.

"Fog," he said. "Thick as your head."

Foxes Court had vanished; London had vanished, as if in an evil dream. "Turn left," said he, pointing into the grimy nothingness with a smirk. "Keep on to the end. Then right, then left again. Cross over Chick Lane and take the first passage on your right. That'll bring you to the Horse Boy . . . or the Tower of London, or the bottom of the River Thames."

He shut the door and I noticed that some of the fog had got into the house and rendered the stairs, the walls and even him, indistinct. His smirk broadened, as if he was proud of it all.

I asked him if the fog was likely to last for long, as I had to meet somebody at the Horse Boy at eight o'clock.

He told me that he'd known fogs last for three days; but some went away in half an hour. He told me that fogs might be patchy and I could walk for five minutes and come right out, into the clear. But equally, I might walk for five hours, and then bang into the tree in the middle of Foxes Court.

I might be lucky and not be robbed and murdered as soon as I stepped outside the door; or I might be unlucky and be knocked on the head in the middle of a streetful of people who'd hear me scream and say: "What was that?"

He rubbed his hands together as if he was entirely satisfied with the misery he had produced in me; and that if there was anything further he could do, in the way of blasting my last hope and encouraging me to weep and kill myself, he was only too willing to oblige.

"Seed!" came a shout. "Mr. Seed, please! Top floor!"

He went into his box and I hid in his cupboard, as I feared that it might have been Mr. Needleman or Mr. K'Nee coming down.

When he came back, I asked him who it had been?

"Mr. Jenkins," he said. "Old K'Nee's clerk."

I began to cry. I couldn't help it. My only hope had been to wait in the house until Mr. Jenkins came down. Now he was gone, into the filthy, sulphurous fog

"Never mind," said the dwarf, his spirits continuing to rise proportionately to the sinking of mine, rather like the great black weight that balanced his hoist. "I'll take you to the Horse Boy. It'll cost you a sixpence, mind. But you can afford it, being so much richer than me!"

At five o'clock, Mr. Seed put on his diminutive coat and his very large hat, remarking that the size of his brain required it; and led me out into the fog.

It should have been dark outside, or nearly so; but somehow the night seemed to be having no better luck in penetrating the air than anything else. It was still of a dirty yellowish gray, very unwholesome for the eyes, nose, and mouth.

Mr. Seed had taken a stick with him—a short, villainous-looking cudgel; and I held one end of it while he voyaged ahead.

"Careful, now! Careful!" he kept calling out, as various lost lawyers and murderers loomed by. "Got me a little boy with me! Careful of the child!"

This seemed to please him—cutting me down in size, I mean; whenever people made him out, and were naturally startled, they looked behind him for something even smaller, about the size of a dog.

Although, as he never tired of telling me, he was four times as old as me and forty times as clever, I think he was rather childish, too; as he enjoyed playing tricks in the fog and bewildering people with his size.

He seemed to have no difficulty in finding his way about, even though everybody else seemed lost. He recognized people when they were nothing, or, at the most, faint stains in the murky air.

"Evening, Mr. Charles! What a night, eh?"

"Is that you, Mr. Seed?"

"That's me, Mr. Charles! Don't make a move or you'll tread on my head!"

Then he was away, chuckling happily:

"He'll be there for hours now, wondering where I am!"

He took me into an alehouse—a favorite place of his. It wasn't the Horse Boy, but, as he explained, there was plenty of time for that, and the fog made him thirsty and I could, if I liked, buy him a pint of ale.

The fog was in the alehouse, too, and made a phantom of the aproned waiter, with his graveyard cough and reddened eyes.

"First of all, Mr. Walker, I want you to meet me friend. He's a hundred and four if he's a day."

The waiter smiled.

"Straight up, Mr. Walker! Look at him! He's a taller dwarf than me!"

The waiter sniggered.

"You will have your little joke, Mr. Seed; meaning, of course, no reflection on your size!"

"A pint, Mr. Walker, and a piece of your best pie for me friend; for I think he's going to faint if he don't get more inside him than the fog."

When the waiter had gone, the dwarf asked me my name. I told him.

"Jones?" he repeated. "Are you sure it's not Smith, or Robinson, like the rest of our customers in Foxes Court?"

He was, it seemed, so used to concealment, that he took it as a matter of course and I had the greatest difficulty in persuading him that Jones was my real name and not just a plain wrapper for the Duke of Clerkenwell or something like that.

"Seed," he said at length. "My name's Hampstead Seed. Hampstead because that's where I was born; and Seed because I might have grown if I'd fallen on better soil."

He stretched out his stubby legs, his stubby arms and his stubby fingers and gazed at them with every appearance of satis faction.

"I've got nothing to hide," he said abruptly; and, I thought, meaning to have a slight dig at me. "All me deformity's out in the open and on public show. So why should I hide the best?"

If, by the best, he meant his disagreeable habit of making people feel uncomfortable, then I felt that there was every reason for him to hide it; but I think he meant his feelings and his sometimes very clever thoughts.

We stayed in the alehouse for about an hour and a half, during which time I felt more and more that I would like to confide everything in Mr. Seed; but I kept remembering Mr. K'Nee's advice, to keep something in reserve, to hold something back. So I kept everything back, except that the person I was to meet in the Horse Boy was Mr. Jenkins, the clerk.

"Mr. Jenkins?" said the dwarf, rather dryly, I thought. "So it's Mr. Jenkins, is it!"

I said: "Yes. He's promised to—" I stopped, remembering Mr. K'Nee again.

"To what? Promised to introduce you at Court? Promised to make you Lord Mayor?"

My feelings of wanting to confide in Mr. Seed vanished, as he turned malicious again.

"He's promised to help me," I said, as coolly as I could.

"So he's promised to help you . . . just like that! Out of the blue! And behind his master's back, I fancy."

"And why shouldn't he?" I demanded, feeling angry that the dwarf was trying to undermine my only hope.

"Oh nothing, nothing! Mr. Jenkins is a fine, upstanding young fellow. At least eight feet tall!"

I could guess why he didn't like Mr. Jenkins. Although he'd said that he didn't care about his queer deformity, I think that he really did. I think he was angry that somebody else was going to help me; and particularly a tall smart person like Mr. K'Nee's clerk. Mr. Seed, no matter how much he grinned and joked, was eaten up with envy inside.

I thought that this was a very bad quality in him; and I felt awkward and embarrassed that I'd found it out.

He guided me to the Horse Boy without another word. We got there at half-past seven and Mr. Jenkins hadn't yet arrived.

"Where are you going to sleep tonight, Jones?"

I felt suddenly alarmed. I hadn't thought of that at all.

I began to say that I supposed I could find a room somewhere; when Mr. Seed asked curtly:

"How much money have you got, Jones?"

I had six pounds and twelve shillings and was about to say so; when once again I remembered the need to keep something back.

"About three pounds," I said.

The dwarf smiled contemptuously.

"Not very clever at counting, are we! I saw six gold guineas in your purse."

I felt myself going very red and tried to think of an excuse.

"Never mind, never mind!" said Mr. Seed. "Just give me the sixpence you owe me."

He began to move away. We were outside the door of the Horse Boy and, for some reason, he wouldn't go inside.

"Tell you what, Jones," he said, coming back. "I'll look in at half-past nine . . . just in case that fine, upstanding young fellow Jenkins hasn't fixed you up. Or you haven't been knocked on the head," he added; and, with a harsh little laugh, vanished into the fog.

I stared after him with great misgivings. I suspected he didn't like me and I thought he'd been altogether too sharp about counting my money.

I hoped that Mr. Jenkins would fix me up; as the dwarf's laugh had sounded decidedly malevolent and I didn't like to think of him creeping back in the dark.

7

THE HORSE BOY HIMSELF was a painted wooden figure, about the height of Mr. Seed, dressed in blue and white striped trousers, and a short blue jacket with enormous yellow buttons. He stood just inside the door, holding out a tray on which were several folded pieces of paper and cards.

I found out after, that these were messages that customers left each other, to the effect that Mr. So-and-So would be back in half an hour, or on Tuesday next at nine.

This steady employment, and, I suppose, the thought that he was of use to the world, seemed to make the Horse Boy very happy, as he wore the largest and the shiniest grin I have ever seen.

Everybody patted him affectionately when they came in and stopped to finger through the contents of the tray; consequently he was rather smooth and worn on top, as if, young as he was, he was going as bald as an egg.

The waiter, who had eyed me very doubtfully at first, as soon as he learned that I was to meet Mr. Jenkins, gave a grin that was the brother of the Horse Boy's, and conducted me to Mr. Jenkins's private seat which was in a cubby-hole beside the fire.

After that, he drifted about the parlor and, whenever he caught my eye, he grinned again.

There must have been about twenty people in the parlor, mostly rather well-dressed young men; and all of them, one way or another, seemed to have been affected by the Horse Boy's grin.

At first, I felt miserably uncomfortable and thought they were all laughing at me, because they could see I was straight from the country and knew nothing about the town; but then I began to feel that it was something else altogether and was being produced by the warmly glowing parlor itself, as if the architect, when he thought of it, had been laughing all the time.

Perhaps even the Horse Boy himself had once been crying his eyes out, and had only begun to grin when he arrived.

After some minutes of staring at him, and at the door beyond, I, too, found myself smiling; though God alone knew that I had little enough cause. Having pinned all my hopes on Mr. Diamond's son being able to take his dead father's place, I now began to think that a boy, perhaps not much older than myself, was not likely to be much use at all. Perhaps, I thought gloomily, he knew nothing of the old business; perhaps he'd never heard of David Jones.

I took out my watch the author of my misery—and wound it up. It was ten minutes to eight and I feared that Mr. Jenkins wouldn't come. At five minutes to eight, I was sure of it; and at eight o'clock I abandoned all hope.

He came at five past—an angel in a blue coat that came up to his ears.

He'd brought a friend with him, and my heart thumped excitedly as I thought that this must be Mr. Diamond's son.

Mr. Jenkins saw me and waved; then, as if to put me in further suspense, he and his friend patted the Horse Boy and read through all the messages with the greatest of care.

The friend was rather taller than Mr. Jenkins; and, when he slipped off his coat, more expensively dressed. There was quite a glitter about him; and when he smiled, it made you think of gold teeth. He whistled and hummed all the time, that old song, "The Miller of Dee." He looked as if he was a year or two older than Mr. Jenkins, which I found surprising, having been prepared for a boy.

At last they came towards me and I jumped up to greet them.

" 'Ere 'e is. This is David Jones's son," said Mr. Jenkins to his friend; and then to me: "This is Mr. Robinson, young feller-me-lad. Mr. Robinson, meet David Jones's son! And vice versa, of course."

"Pleased to have the honor!" said Mr. Robinson, and shook my hand which had gone quite limp with disappointment.

Mr. Robinson's grip was firm, and a heavy ring he was wearing dug into my palm rather painfully. He went on whistling: "*I care for nobody, no, not I . . .*"

"Cheer up, young feller-me-lad!" said Mr. Jenkins, seeing my dejection. "It's Mr. Robinson what knows old Diamond's son. Ain't that so, old man?"

Mr. Robinson nodded and he and Mr. Jenkins squeezed down beside me. They both smelled of the fog. Mr. Robinson stopped whistling and began to hum.

"So you're old Jones's son?" he said when he came to the end of the verse, gazing at me with a warm interest. "Spitting image, eh, old man?" he said to Mr. Jenkins; and went on humming.

They each seemed to talk of everybody as old, as if they themselves were the youngest and brightest things in creation.

"Did you know my father, sir?" I asked eagerly.

"Know him? Know old Jones? What do you take me for! Methuselah? It must be all of twenty years since old David Jones was in these parts!"

"It's just 'is joke," said Mr. Jenkins, noticing that I'd gone red. " 'E's all right when you get to know 'im! Come on, Robinson! This young feller-me-lad 'as just lost 'is pa and run away from—from—Where was it you said you came from?"

"From—from the country," I said, uncomfortably remembering Mr. K'Nee. I was determined to keep as much as possible to myself until I found Mr. Diamond's son; although the strain was beginning to tell.

"That's right. From the country," said Mr. Jenkins, beaming at Mr. Robinson. "Let's 'ave a drink on it!"

He snapped his fingers with a noise like a gun going off, and asked the waiter to bring two pints and a half of the Horse Boy's best. While the waiter was gone, Mr. Robinson hummed and whistled that he cared for nobody and nobody cared for him. He looked quite pleased about it. The Horse Boy's best arrived and turned out to be sherry.

We drank and I asked Mr. Robinson what Mr. Diamond's son was like, and when could I expect to see him? Mr. Robinson promised that it would be in two, or possibly three shakes of a lamb's tail; the only trouble was, that John Diamond wasn't that easy to find. He came and went, so to speak, like the fog. He wasn't exactly mysterious; but he was inclined to drift.

"Is he very poor?" I asked, thinking of some ragged waif who would shine like a star when I told him who I was and that I wanted to restore to him everything his father had lost.

I imagined taking him back to Woodbury, and my mother

adopting him and bringing him up as an extra Jones. I thought of going to school with him . . .

"Poor? Depends what you mean by poor," said Mr. Robinson, leaning forward and examining my watch and purse which were both on the table.

I had, by the way, paid for the sherry as I wanted to give a good impression; and I couldn't get the purse back in my pocket without digging my elbows into my two companions.

"He's not as rich as you. No gold watch, no gold guineas. No good coat; no strong, country shoes. He's not as well fed as you. He's not as well provided for as you. But poor? I wouldn't call him poor. Just needy. Was it in your mind to help him with anything?"

"Of course it was!" said Mr. Jenkins. "Told you so, Robinson! It's all about that ten thousand pounds my owner was on about!"

Mr. Jenkins had a habit of referring to his employer as his owner, as if Mr. K'Nee kept a racing stable and Mr. Jenkins was his fleetest horse.

"I don't know anything about that money!" I cried. "Really I don't!"

"He don't know!" said Mr. Jenkins cheerfully. "He came all the way from—from. Where did you say?"

"From the country."

"All the way from the country to see me owner in Foxes Court to find old Diamond, and 'e don't know a thing!"

"I don't! I don't!"

"Then what is it you want with old Diamond's son . . . with John?"

"I—I just wanted to—to tell him my father's died! His father was a—a friend! My father told me . . . just—just before he died!"

This seemed to amuse Mr. Jenkins even more. He began to

laugh rather squeakily, and even Mr. Robinson began to chuckle and I found myself being pumped and squeezed between them until I felt sick. I could see the Horse Boy grinning wider than ever; and suddenly there was the waiter with more sherry and I was paying and he was enjoying the joke, too.

I wondered what it was; I wondered what I could have said that was so extraordinarily funny that I didn't understand.

"Told him before he died!" spluttered Jenkins. "Before he kicked the bucket! Oh my! That's rich! Before 'e went into liquidation! Bankrupt! Carey Street!"

This last idea seemed too much for Mr. Jenkins altogether and he was compelled to bury his face in his tankard and leave his shaking shoulders to express his high amusement.

I sat there feeling unutterably bewildered, ashamed and wildly angry, too, with this uncanny world of digs and hints and smartness, where everything turned out to be a joke in the end . . . even death.

I wanted to get up and run away; but the fog outside had imprisoned me. I longed, even, for the malicious dwarf to come back; but it was not yet nine o'clock. I hated Mr. Jenkins, and I was frightened of him, too. I knew he only wanted the secret of the ten thousand pounds, which he thought I had; and he'd stop Mr. Robinson helping me if he didn't get it.

Then Mr. Robinson said:

"That's enough, Jenkins, old man. That's quite enough of that."

To my astonishment, Mr. Jenkins stopped laughing as if he'd been punched. I don't think that Mr. Jenkins ever forgot that Mr. Robinson was his superior and that he was rather lucky to have him as a friend.

"The trouble with you, Jenkins, is that you've got no feelings."

"I—I beg your pardon, old man?"

Mr. Robinson turned to me; and suddenly I felt that he wasn't at all like Mr. Jenkins. In fact, he was really quite gentlemanly. I felt that he liked me and was angry both with Mr. Jenkins and himself over the little joke. He smiled faintly; and I was aware of a curiously warm feeling between us; a sense of sharing something from which Mr. Jenkins had just been excluded. I suppose it was breeding.

"You may not know it, Jenkins," he said, "but feelings can be very strong. Feelings can quite easily drive a boy to run away from—from the country. Feelings can drive a boy to find out his dead father's friend. It don't have to be money, Jenkins. Feelings are quite enough. Feelings can be very deep, Jenkins. Feelings can be as deep as—"

"Hell?" suggested Jenkins.

"The River Thames," corrected Mr. Robinson.

"At London Bridge, old man?"

"At London Bridge . . . old man."

I finished my drink, and back came the waiter with more. As far as I know, nobody called for him, but there he was, beaming and waiting for his money. I paid.

Mr. Robinson said, ignoring Mr. Jenkins completely:

"Come back tomorrow, young Jones. I'll do what I can to find John Diamond. I can't promise, of course. But I'll do what I can. Feelings must be respected, eh?"

"What time? What time, sir?"

"Make it five o'clock. If I'm not here, I'll leave a note with Jimmy." He indicated that "Jimmy" was the Horse Boy, and the note would be on his tray.

I thanked Mr. Robinson with tears in my eyes; and in order to hide my emotion, I finished the rest of my drink. I put down the tankard, which Mr. Jenkins thoughtfully refilled from his own.

"If—if you find him, sir, will you b-bring him with you?"

Mr. Robinson reminded me that John Diamond was a needy fellow and did not go much in places like the Horse Boy. John Diamond's haunts were on the darker side of the town. John Diamond, being a bit seedy, didn't care much to be dragged out into the light of day.

I gazed round the parlor, which Mr. Robinson evidently took as being representative of the light of day. It was rather hazy and more full of cubby-holes than I'd recollected. They looked like the work of enormous mice.

I shuddered and drank some more sherry. Then I stared hard at Jimmy, and thought of tomorrow at five.

The Horse Boy appeared to be winking at me, first with one eye and then with the other. I thought about it carefully, and then winked back. I caught sight of Mr. Jenkins beginning to snigger.

"I'm quite all right," I said.

"Of course you're all right," said Mr. Robinson.

"I'm more all right than him," I said, pointing to Mr. Jenkins.

Mr. Robinson agreed, and then, with appalling suddenness, he and Mr. Jenkins slid up over the top of the table and left me on the floor.

"Where's he gone?" I heard Mr. Jenkins say. "One minute he was sitting there, now 'e's gone."

I did not think it necessary to answer, as I could see Mr. Jenkins's feet quite distinctly.

"Passed out," said Mr. Jenkins. "Cold."

I lay quite still. I was comfortable where I was and thought it better not to move until I had had a rest. I could hear Mr. Robinson humming and whistling and vague snatches of conversation going on over my head. I thought it was very like lying in bed and listening to voices downstairs; only the other way round, of course.

Mostly I heard Mr. Jenkins, as his voice was higher and carried more.

" 'E knows . . . 'e knows all right . . . John Diamond . . . must know . . . cryin', 'e was!"

Then Mr. Robinson, very indistinct.

"Have to see what Diamond says . . . good old John!"

There was a sound of laughing; and then Mr. Jenkins again:

"London Bridge, eh? Me owner won't 'alf cut up rough about that . . ."

"Make it Blackfriars, then. It's feelings, Jenkins, feelings . . . no accounting for 'em . . . very queer . . ."

"Not so queer as old John . . . ten thousand . . . set me up for life . . . John ought to 'and over, eh? . . . What d'you say . . ."

"You know old John!"

"Good old John . . . John . . . John . . ."

The name went trundling off into a loud dark roaring; and then there were faces, some laughing, some angry, and one that was huge, ugly and malign. At the same time, I felt such a blast of hatred, that all the world went black; and there was nothing left but a whistling:

"I care for nobody, no, not I;
And nobody cares for me!"

8

I HAD A HORRIBLE nightmare. I dreamed that my father was dead; that I was in a strange place far from my home; that I had been told of a great sum of money and forgotten where it was; that I was searching for somebody enormously important and that he was hiding from me; that suddenly there had been a blast of hatred strong enough to murder me; and that I had been confronted by a glaring face as ugly as it was malign.

Then I found out that it hadn't been a dream. The malign face had come back. It was less ugly—it was rather refined, in fact—but it was no less malign. It was the face of the dwarf.

In addition, I *was* in a strange place, under a strange ceiling and surrounded by strange walls. I seemed to be confined in something like a coffin; and the smallest movement provoked a sharp pain in my head as if a drunken undertaker had been knocking nails into it under the impression it was the lid. I felt very ill.

"Where—where am I?" I moaned.

"In St. Paul's Cathedral," said Mr. Seed contemptuously. "And I'm the Dean."

When I expressed timid disbelief, he informed me that I was in his bed, in his house, which was situated in Hanging Sword Alley, off Fleet Street. I had slept away the night and owed him a shilling for his hospitality.

The mention of money made me feel even more uneasy, until he produced my purse and my watch and laid them on my chest.

"Found them on the table," he said. "And found you under it."

I opened my purse. The dwarf watched me.

"It's all there. Six pounds and two shillings. You're still rich."

I gave him his shilling and tried to sit up. The pain was terrible. Mr. Seed grinned and assured me that, in an hour or so, the worst effects of my drinking too much would have worn off; whereas now I might feel as if I had been run over by a coach and six, I might confidently look forward to feeling that it had only been a coach and pair.

"Am—am I far away?" I asked, remembering that I had an appointment with the Horse Boy at five o'clock.

"Where from?"

"The Horse Boy."

"Half a mile as the crow flies. But longer as the dwarf and drunken boy weaved."

I said I was sorry for the trouble I had caused. Mr. Seed put the shilling in his pocket and said I had paid him for it.

"I've got to be back at the Horse Boy," I said unhappily, "at—"

"At five o'clock," said the dwarf.

"How did you know?"

"You told me. Don't you remember?"

I shook my head, which now seemed to have a cannonball inside it that rolled frightfully.

"Don't you remember our little walk?" pursued Mr. Seed, sitting down on a dwarf-sized stool by the bed and resting his short hands on his stubby knees. "Don't you remember falling asleep in the roadway? Don't you remember trying to walk through a wall and crying because you couldn't?"

I confessed that these episodes, together with others of a similar kind, had been expunged from my mind.

"Don't you remember the footsteps?"

"What footsteps?"

"The footsteps in the fog. Shuffle—drag . . . shuffle—drag . . . shuffle—drag! That's how you said they went."

I felt as cold as ice.

"D-did you hear them? Did—did you *see* anybody?"

"No. But you did. Heard 'em at every corner. Don't you remember?"

"No . . . no."

"That's queer. That's very queer," said the dwarf, thoughtfully.

"Why?"

"You made such a yelling commotion about it. I thought, once or twice, that you really could see the man . . . the way you stared and glared."

"W-what did I see?"

"I told you, I never saw more than a green boy. A very green boy," he added, with a malicious smile.

"Was there anything—anything else?"

"Only your shouting out about Mr. Diamond being dead and that it wasn't your fault. I wondered if you could have seen the name painted up."

"What name?"

"Diamond. I told you, Diamond."

"Where?"

"Round in Fleet Street. Jones and Diamond. Coffee Merchants. This house used to be part of it before the business was sold. Mr. Twiss bought it up and kept the name for the goodwill.

This house belongs to Mr. K'Nee. He's me landlord and takes me rent."

Mr. Seed stood up.

"And talking of Mr. K'Nee, it's time I was off to me place of business. It's eight o'clock."

I begged him to stay a little longer and tell me more about Jones and Diamond. He frowned and then, recalling that my name was Jones, wondered if there was any connection between me and the Jones round the other side.

I told him that I was sure that there was. My father had indeed been in coffee and Mr. Diamond had been his partner. I asked the dwarf if he remembered my father? He shook his head. The business had changed hands long before he'd come to Hanging Sword Alley. Jones and Diamond were only faded names to him.

Nevertheless he said that if I was interested in visiting my father's old place of business, I might stroll round into Fleet Street and take a cup of coffee in the shop that Mr. Twiss had opened in the front of the old warehouse. Otherwise I might remain in his bed until four o'clock, when he would be back to take me to the Horse Boy—in exchange for another sixpence, of course.

He left me strongly advising the coffee; which, if I wanted to keep secrets, he said, I would be better advised to drink than sherry. After that, he banged the door and thumped down the stairs, exchanging loud good mornings with other inhabitants of the house.

I lay back in his short, narrow bed, wondering wretchedly what else I had shouted out in the night. Had I shouted about Hertford and Woodbury and my Uncle Turner? I wondered if the dwarf had gone off to inform on me in the hope of a reward. Certainly he was a greedy little man as far as money was concerned, and I knew that he disliked me for being richer than him.

Later I had cause to remember this fear; but at that time my greatest concern was over the footsteps in the fog. That I'd heard them and couldn't remember them, somehow made them more frightening; and I wondered what else was hidden inside my head.

I got out of bed and staggered a good deal. Not because of illness, but because the floor sloped in several different directions, so that even water, I think, would have had difficulty in finding its own level. It was an ancient house that had shrunk and sunk and tortured its doors and windows into the most fearful problems in geometry.

I thought of my schoolmaster in Hertford, and how he would have delighted in making constructions on them; and then, when I didn't understand, beaten me till the dust flew out like a carpet.

It was Friday, and I would have been sitting in my place at school. At once a new rush of strangeness came over me as if I had not run away all at once, but part by part, and with each part came a fresh loss. I missed all the old, familiar sounds of my home; and I thought of my mother and sisters frantic with worry. My heart warmed greatly towards them and I shed several melancholy tears as I thought of myself as the beloved ornament of the household, lost forever.

I went to the window and looked out, to see what had taken the place of grass and trees.

The fog had gone and in its place was a misty sunshine, tattered with black smoke. Below me stretched Hanging Sword Alley, a long straight lane, thin as a sword blade, cutting downhill between buildings and ending with a blazing slice of the River Thames.

I saw small boats and sunken barges drifting, it seemed, out of one house and vanishing into another, at about the level of the second floor. I opened the window and gazed round at the furrowed fields of roofs from which a million chimneys sprouted like stricken corn.

I stared on them with gloomy awe; till, leaning out for a wider view towards my left, I saw, with a kind of shock, an immense dark mountain heaving up over the town and sitting in the sky.

It was the dome of St. Paul's Cathedral; and I had never seen anything so huge.

Absolutely lost in wonderment, I tried to imagine the tiny London workmen building it up, stone by stone, until it got so high that people begged them to stop. But higher and higher they went until at last the master-builder screwed in the golden cross on top, like a locking-pin; and there was St. Paul's finished, and a wonder of the world.

Feeling cold, I shut the window and looked round for my clothes, as I was only in my shirt. I found them folded on a chair. I noticed that my other shirt and a pair of my stockings were missing. I felt alarmed and angry that the dwarf should have stolen from me while I slept.

I began to dress, feeling that the sooner I left his house, the safer I would feel, when there came a knock on the door. It was followed immediately by the appearance of a red face tied up in a cloth, like a pudding.

"Mrs. Carwardine, first floor front," announced the face. "Only popped up to tell that Mr. Seed give me your linen and stockin's for washin'. Cost you fruppence; but 'e said you got money to pay."

She vanished, leaving me to change my mind about the dwarf.

He wasn't a thief, but he was a real demon for emptying my purse.

Feeling a little easier in my mind that I hadn't fallen among thieves, I finished dressing and was about to leave the room, when I was thrown into a fresh alarm.

There was the most enormous bang that shook the whole house till its very teeth rattled.

I thought we must have been blown up and rushed to the door to escape before the building crashed in ruins. I could hear a violent commotion on the stairs, then more banging and the sound of smashing glass. Mercifully the house remained standing.

Mrs. Carwardine had begun shouting and shrieking at the top of her voice: "Boarders! Boarders!" and a bell began to ring as if a mad muffin-man had got inside and was determined to sell all his stock.

"Boarders! Boarders!" yelled Mrs. Carwardine, and several more female voices joined in.

I ran back to look out of the window. Down below, in the alley, a dozen or more ragged boys—some of them quite big—were hurling bricks and stones at the dwarf's house and making ready to thunder at the door again with a great piece of timber.

"Boarders! Boarders!" shrieked the women; and I saw, coming out from between the slits and cracks that intersected the crowding tenements, as if they were falling apart at the seams, a grim and menacing pack of ruffians, with murder in their eyes.

There was something about them, and the awful darkness from which they emerged, that strongly suggested wolves and bears coming out of a forest. Although they seemed to be armed with nothing worse than fists, I felt that they had sharp claws and even sharper teeth.

Instantly the ragged boys dropped their weapons and fled. Mrs. Carwardine came out into the alley, still holding the bell.

"Much obliged—much obliged," she said. "Sorry to have troubled you so early. But very much obliged . . . on be'alf of Mr. Seed, naturally."

The wolves and bears grinned, displaying horrible teeth, and went back into their forest; and Mrs. Carwardine came back into the house.

I stared down Hanging Sword Alley to see if the boys would dare to come back again. But they had gone. There was a moment of quietness; then I heard, from a little way off, a strangely familiar sound. It was somebody whistling.

"I care for nobody, no, not I;
And nobody cares for me!"

9

WHAT WAS MR. ROBINSON doing out there? A thousand thoughts rushed into my mind and came together and made one. Mr. Robinson had found John Diamond and was coming to tell me!

But how did he know I was in the dwarf's house? Instantly I was plunged into gloom. His presence was nothing to do with me. I turned away from the window.

But of course he knew where I was! He must have seen Mr. Seed take me away last night; and Mr. Seed was well-known to his friend, Mr. Jenkins! So he *was* out there on my account! And any moment he would be knocking on the front door.

I left the room and hurried down the stairs to be ready for him. There was a crowd in the hall. Everybody in the house was out there, talking excitedly about the damage that had just been done, which amounted to a couple of broken windows and some largish splinters out of the door.

There was so much noise, mostly from a tremendous number of children, that I feared that Mr. Robinson's knock would go unheard. I tried to push my way through; and Mrs. Carwardine, catching sight of me, bundled some of the children out of the way—which was rather like trying to push water as they all kept flowing back again—and introduced me, at the top of her voice, as "Mr. Seed's young gentleman," to two other ladies: a Mrs. Baynim and a Mrs. Branch.

Mrs. Carwardine thought I'd been meaning to go outside and she strongly advised against it, on account of "them ragged boys" who might still be hanging about.

Before I could tell her that I was expecting somebody to call on me, she said, all in one breath, that it was shocking awful that them boys never came when there was men in the house to give them what for, such as Mr. Seed and Mr. Carwardine—

"And Mr. Baynim," put in Mrs. Baynim sharply. Mrs. Branch merely looked hopeful.

—Mr. Carwardine being a Thames waterman, continued Mrs. Carwardine, flowing round the interruption as if it had been a small pebble, and you know what *they* are, and if I looked down

Hanging Sword Alley at eleven o'clock, I might see him wave as he rowed by.

She paused to hit one of the children, who I supposed was her own, and demand that they shouldn't disgrace the house in front of Mr. Seed's young gentleman.

Mrs. Carwardine, apart from being immensely talkative, was a very anxious and polite person and thought me very grand. She made a great deal of my shirt that she was washing (her arms were covered with grayish soap and there was some on her forehead), and said it was of the very best quality and she doubted if you might get finer, even in Gracechurch Street. She supposed I must be worth a mint of money and she hoped I wouldn't be offended if she showed Mrs. Baynim and Mrs. Branch my stockings, too.

Mrs. Baynim, whose head was also done up like a pudding, and who had moles all over her face like currants, did not seem impressed. She was, I thought, one of those haughty women who always disparages boys. But Mrs. Branch, who was thin and gypsyish, eyed me with even greater respect than did Mrs. Carwardine.

Mrs. Baynim remarked that she couldn't waste the morning standing in the hall like a common gossip, and withdrew, taking a quantity of children with her, apparently at random. I never did discover for certain, which were Baynims and which were Branches. Mrs. Carwardine was easier, as she had two daughters of about my age who were always screaming at each other.

Mrs. Carwardine apologized for Mrs. Baynim whose husband was in the building trade and came from Shropshire. Then she hit one of her noisy daughters again and told Mrs. Branch that I'd come over queer last night and Mr. Seed himself had brought me back.

Mrs. Branch peered at me timidly and said that I *did* look rather peaky and she hoped she wasn't taking a liberty but might she offer me some hot soup and cheese?

I hesitated, for I was still waiting for Mr. Robinson to knock; but Mrs. Branch took it the wrong way and overwhelmed me with apologies for having presumed and hoped that I hadn't taken offense because she'd offered me soup just as if I was an ordinary person instead of being somebody rather princely who wore a shirt that might have come from Gracechurch Street.

She didn't exactly say all that, but she made me feel it and I didn't know what to say. Mrs. Carwardine wasn't any help as she, who had already been staggered by my shirt and stockings, was enlarging on the quality of my coat.

I told Mrs. Branch that I would be pleased to take soup with her; and she went off with her children—there were three of them—looking so honored that I felt like a bishop.

Mrs. Carwardine, addressing her two daughters, who were sitting on the stairs, one above the other, and making faces at me, declared that I was a kind and condescending person whose example ought to be followed.

This made me feel very strange and I began to think that my family had never really understood me as they had always tended to the opposite view, that my example was not so much to be followed as caught up with and stopped.

Mrs. Carwardine told me, all in one breath again, that Mrs. Branch was a good soul underneath, except that she was inclined to be light-headed from hope. She had tramped all the way from

York with her children, looking for her husband who was either a soldier, a sailor or a traveling salesman in saucepans; she wasn't quite sure. He'd gone to London and she kept seeing him down every street; so that hardly a day went by without Mrs. Branch saying that, if only she'd been able to run across the road without being knocked down, she'd have been united, and that Mr. Branch had put on a lot of weight.

She paused for another breath, and I listened for the sound of Mr. Robinson's knock while the upper of Mrs. Carwardine's daughters tried to kick her sister off the lower stair. No knock came; and I guessed that Mr. Robinson, seeing the savage boys, had gone away and would come back later.

"If you want to step outside, dear," said Mrs. Carwardine, seeing me look at the door, "I expect it will be all right now."

I thanked her—which piece of good breeding did not go unrecommended to the two Miss Carwardines, who promptly began squeaking thank-yous at each other like spiteful mice.

Mrs. Carwardine picked up a heavy broom and, for a moment, I thought she was going to batter her children; but instead, she went to the back of the hall and thumped loudly on the wall.

"That'll learn you!" she shouted with each thump. "Pig! Villain! Coward!"

After a moment, there came an answering thump and a furious voice shouted back that he would have the law on her.

She put down the broom and returned to the foot of the stairs

"It's only that Mr. Twiss, dear," she said. "Mr. Twiss, from the Coffee. He's be'ind it, all right."

I thought she meant the wall—which in point of fact he was, behind it, I mean—but it turned out that she was referring to the ferocious attack of the ragged boys.

"It's these premises, dear," she said. "That Mr. Twiss wants to get poor Mr. Seed out. It ain't anything personal, really, it's just business. You see, he needs the premises for hisself on account of havin' no back way in for deliveries, so all them barrels and sacks has to come round the front and upset all his fine gentlemen at their coffee. And if I catch you nicking sugar from there again, I'll have the hide off you and so will Mr. Carwardine!"

This last was directed at the two Miss Carwardines who had suddenly become friends and were clasping each other round the waist.

"Yes, dear," she went on to me. "It's just business. Mr. Seed, workin' as he does, in Foxes Court, and knowin' a thing or two, has got what you call a lease. That means Mr. Twiss can't get him out exceptin' by things like them boys. But Mr. Seed knows his rights, and, boys or no boys, he won't stir. He's very obstinate, is Mr. Seed. For a little man, he's very obstinate indeed!"

"Soup!" screamed Mrs. Branch from above. "If the young gentleman would step up, please! Soup!"

The two Miss Carwardines curtsied unexpectedly as Mrs. Carwardine led me past them and up the stairs, talking indiscriminately all the time.

"That's nice, girls. Mr. Carwardine will be pleased when I tell him. Mrs. Branch lives very humble of course . . . These stairs is horrible dirty, I must mention it to Mrs. Baynim . . . What with havin' no husband to speak of, and havin' to live off stitchin' and sewin', which don't bring in much . . . And if I catch you nickin' her pins again, you'll not sit down for a fortnight . . . Well, here he is, Mrs. Branch! Mr. Seed's young gentleman as large as life!"

Mrs. Branch's room was a real bewilderment of ragged old clothes hanging up everywhere so that you had to duck and dodge to get by them. It was very hard not to tread on the little Branches, who were all very thin and would probably have snapped, like twigs; and even harder to find somewhere to sit down.

"Over here, Mr. Seed's young gentleman!" cried Mrs. Branch, appearing from behind an ancient green coat, like a tree fairy.

She drew aside a tattered article that I supposed might have been a petticoat, and had a hole through it as if a cannonball had passed that way, and revealed a chair. I sat down, rather jerkily, as I expected pins.

"Will you take your cheese before your soup, or as afters, Mr. Seed's young gentleman?" inquired Mrs. Branch.

I told her I didn't mind. This threw her into such a state of confusion that she had to appeal to Mrs. Carwardine, whose head appeared through the hole in the petticoat.

"Mrs. Branch wants to know, dear, if you wants your soup before your cheese?"

I told her, yes; and both heads went away, leaving me entirely curtained in among Mrs. Branch's hanging work. It was very odd, sitting there with no idea where anybody was, until a waistcoat, or a dressing-gown twitched aside and revealed one of the Miss Carwardines mincing past, fantastically dressed in borrowed rags with battered feathers in her hair.

My soup arrived. I was the only one who had any, and I felt quite regal, alone in my tent and being waited on. I'm sorry to say, I rather looked down on the children; and I think that, if I myself had been present, I would have looked down on me, too . . . if you know what I mean.

At eleven o'clock—Mr. Robinson still not having called—I was invited to accompany Mrs. Carwardine downstairs and out into Hanging Sword Alley to see Mr. Carwardine—a tiny figure in a tiny boat—wave as he rowed by. Then I went back for my cheese.

But before that, I looked towards the tenements from which the ruffians had come that morning and frightened the ragged boys away. They were tall and toppling buildings and I saw a thin slit between them that vanished, under a line of washing, into a menacing blackness.

"You don't want to go in there, dear," said Mrs. Carwardine, drawing me back into the house. "It ain't safe in there. Throats is cut in there as soon as spit."

We got back into Mrs. Branch's room and I found my chair again.

"I was tellin' him, Mrs. Branch," said Mrs. Carwardine, "about not goin' in to Whitefriars. I was tellin' him that throats is cut in there."

"I seen a gent go in what never come out," said Mrs. Branch, leaning round the petticoat. "Never seen again."

"Exceptin' in pieces," said Mrs. Carwardine. "They cut 'em up, you know."

"At night," said Mrs. Branch, coming back round the petticoat.

"Mr. Carwardine seen 'em," said Mrs. Carwardine, appearing from behind a coat and going away again.

"I wonder if that's what happened to Mr. Branch?" said Mrs. Branch, vanishing again.

"Oh no, dear. Mr. Carwardine would have found him!"

"Cheese, Mr. Seed's young gentleman! Excuse fingers."

"Like I said, dear," said Mrs. Carwardine, as I ate my cheese, "you don't want to go into Whitefriars."

She was right. I didn't. I remembered the line of washing, and shuddered. I supposed the washing had been done to get out the blood.

"But of course Mr. Seed's all right," said Mrs. Carwardine. "Being a dwarf, and meanin' no offense, but he is a dwarf whichever way you looks at it, he comes and goes in there as he pleases. All them thieves and murderers and footpads never lays a finger on him, exceptin' in the way of good luck. He's their lucky dwarf. That's why they comes out to help him. When them boys comes, Mr. Seed's only got to ring a bell and shout 'Boarders!'— which is a very common expression with pirates—and out they comes, ready and willin' to oblige by slittin' a few throats! I suppose it's nice of 'em, really; but I ain't sure that I'm not more frightened of them murderers than I am of them boys! But it's all business, dear, and beyond me!"

After that, Mrs. Carwardine went away with her daughters to get on with her washing, and left me with Mrs. Branch, who begged me to take some pie. I spent some time trying to persuade her that my name was William, and not Mr. Seed's young gentleman. But she never got further than "Mr. Jones."

At half-past three Mrs. Carwardine and her daughters came up with a jug of ale. Mrs. Branch fetched various peculiar receptacles, distantly related to cups, and the ale was distributed all round. We were sitting drinking it, when Mrs. Branch said abruptly:

"I don't like that tune. It gives me the shivers."

There was silence; and once again I heard the whistling outside.

"I care for nobody, no, not I;
And nobody cares for me!"

It was Mr. Robinson. He had returned. I waited for his knock.

"There's somethin' burnin'!" said Mrs. Carwardine suddenly. "Hope it ain't your stockin's, dear. I'd best go and see . . ."

She stood up; but before she could leave the room, there came the most horrible screech from downstairs, followed by the noise of the front door bursting open. There were more screeches—dreadful agonized ones—and then a violent uproar, as if hundreds of feet were pounding up the stairs!

10

IT WAS MOSTLY Mr. Seed. He had come back early. He had not been expected; and had made a catch. What a catch!

He came puffing and panting into Mrs. Branch's room, shouting:

"Where are you? Where are you all?"

The hanging clothes shook and swayed, as if they wanted to get out of the way of Mr. Seed's catch; as if, patched and smelly and ragged as they were, Mr. Seed's catch was something they wouldn't even touch with a barge-pole; as if Mr. Seed had brought in with him the boiled down essence of all violence, blackness and disease.

"Caught him! Caught him!" shouted the dwarf, holding out at a very short arm's length, and I don't know by what part, a boy.

I say a boy, although he was much more like a wild and savage animal; a largish rat, maybe, in a long black coat that thrashed about round his legs. He had some tufts of reddish hair, which made him look as if somebody had started to burn him down, for reasons of health, and left him smoldering.

To make matters worse, there was some smoke about; but it was coming from a piece of tarred rope that Mr. Seed was holding in his other hand.

"Tried to burn us down!" panted Mr. Seed, waving the glowing rope. "Caught him at it! Trying to push it under the door!"

He shook his catch who promptly screeched and made a sudden twist with the object of biting Mr. Seed anywhere he could. I saw his mouth fly open and display a few ragged teeth and a sharp little tongue. Mr. Seed dropped him instantly and kicked the door shut to stop him getting away.

"Catch him! Catch him!"

At once everything in the room began to flap and swing, like sails at the beginning of a storm, as everybody blundered about after the screeching scuttling boy. Mrs. Carwardine was shrieking, Mrs. Branch's children were howling and the room was absolute bedlam.

"He's here! He's over here!"

"He's gone!"

"He can't! Where—where?"

"There he is! Fetch a poker or something!"

"I've got him!"

"Where are you?"

"Quick! Quick! In the corner! Too late! He's got away again!" The excitement was enormous. It was like hunting a fox.

"I've found him! He's down here! Down behind the chair!"

"Hold on to him! Catch hold of him! By his hair, if you like!"

It was me who found him. I hadn't expected to; and, I admit, I was more than a little frightened when I saw him suddenly. I thought he was going to spring at me. I backed away.

"I told you to catch hold of him!" said Mr. Seed, pushing me out of the way. "Or are you afraid of dirtyin' your hands, Mr. Jones?"

I felt stupid and angry; and wasn't helped by Mrs. Carwardine saying:

"You can't expect it, Mr. Seed, sir. He ain't used to that sort of thing."

The two Miss Carwardines laughed squeakily; and Mrs. Branch, who seemed to have got lost in her own room, suddenly appeared round the side of the torn petticoat, waving an iron poker and shouting:

"Who wanted it? Here it is! Here it is, Mr. Jones!"

She thrust it into my hand, meaning, I suppose, for me to kill the boy with it.

"What's your name?" demanded the dwarf, standing with his stumpy legs astride and his hands on his hips. He was shaking with anger.

The boy spat at him. The two Miss Carwardines nodded approvingly as if for once they'd been confronted by an example they were prepared to follow.

"Who put you up to it?" pursued Mr. Seed. "Burnin' me house down, I mean."

The boy spat again.

"Was it Mr. Twiss from the Coffee?"

The boy looked exceedingly cunning; but somehow I thought he didn't understand, any more than an animal would have understood. I wondered if he could even talk. Mr. Seed, however, thought differently.

"Give me that!" he said, taking the poker out of my hand.

The boy's eyes glinted and he shrank back against the wall.

"Do you want me to beat it out of you?" inquired Mr. Seed, flourishing the poker. "Because I will, you know. There ain't an inch of pity in me. I'm too short for that. Was it Mr. Twiss what paid you? Or was it—"

Suddenly the boy gave the most terrific screech, put his head down and sprang at the dwarf, with his fists going like mad.

He caught Mr. Seed in the chest so that he had to stagger and clutch on to the hanging clothes. They came down all over him in a rush and a large part of the room was exposed, with startled faces looking everywhere.

"The door! The door!" shouted Mr. Seed, much muffled. "Get to the door!"

I saw his arm come up, waving the poker. I took it and rushed across to the door. The scuttling boy, who had knocked Mrs. Carwardine over and left her shouting, had already got his hand on the door-knob.

I lifted the poker, meaning to bring it down on his arm. Or I think I meant to; I don't know, as I was very excited at the time and anxious to make up for not having held on to him before.

He looked straight at me. I've never seen such a look, before or since. I don't know how to describe it. It wasn't fear; it wasn't hatred. Or at least, not in any way I knew them. It was as if—and I can't think of any other way to put it—it was as if a scream had looked at me.

I lowered the poker; and the boy was gone.

Naturally Mr. Seed was very angry with me. I suppose he thought I'd been slow, or frightened of being bitten, or of getting my hands dirty; which, I must say, would have surprised my family . . . the part about getting my hands dirty, I mean.

He stamped up and down the room, getting his head entangled with Mrs. Branch's belongings, and referring to me as Lord Muck. Mrs. Carwardine, who still had a great deal of respect for my shirt and stockings, was rather shocked to hear Mr. Seed abusing me; and in some sort of defense of me, went downstairs and banged on the wall again with the broomstick and shouted:

"Pig! Villain! Coward! Burn us down, would you!"

Back came the banging and the threat of having the law on Mrs. Carwardine. This had the effect of calming Mr. Seed's temper; but he still continued to look at me with a strong dislike.

I thought at first that he would refuse to take me to the Horse Boy out of revenge; but his fondness for money got the better of his feelings; and, at half-past four, he got up and said:

"It's time for your sixpennyworth, Lord Muck."

It was nearly dark when we went out into the alley. The watermen's boats were already lighted, and they drifted past on their reflections, like pairs of fireflies. We began to walk.

"Good evening, Mr. Seed."

"Evenin' . . . evenin' . . ."

"Nice to see you looking so well, Mr. Seed . . ."

"Evenin' . . . evenin' . . ."

"How are things in Foxes Court, Mr. Seed?"

"Mustn't grumble. Up and down . . . up and down . . ."

"You will have your little joke, Mr. Seed!"

He seemed to know everybody; or at least, everybody knew him. We reached the door of the Horse Boy and he demanded his sixpence.

"Shall I come back and fetch you again?"

"I think I can remember the way, Mr. Seed."

He looked rather disappointed to have lost an extra sixpence; but then brightened up when he understood I was going to come back, which meant another shilling, for the night.

"Are you meetin' Mr. Jenkins, or the other one?"

He glanced up at me inquisitively.

"That boy," he said, abruptly changing the subject. "He'd have killed you if he'd had a knife. Wouldn't have thought twice about it."

"I—I'm sorry," I said.

I was confused and uncomfortable as I realized that Mr. Seed had known all the time that I'd let the boy go on purpose. That was why he'd been so angry. I suppose it would have been better if I'd smashed the boy's arm.

I said as much, and he frowned; so I asked him, meaning to excuse myself completely, whether he himself really had been going to beat the boy with the poker. He smiled.

"That's different," he said. "He was a head taller than me. When he was standing up."

"Oh yes, of course," I said sarcastically. "I didn't think of that."

"Of course you didn't, William Jones. You don't think of anything. You may be taller than me, and you may be richer; but always remember, I'm four times as old as you, and forty times as clever. If you see that boy again, run for your life!"

II

THE HORSE BOY GRINNED; the parlor grinned, and so did the waiter. The usual dozen or so smart young men were sitting about in the cubby-holes and at the tables, exactly as they'd been before. I thought they might have been there since last night.

I stood by the door looking round for Mr. Robinson, when the waiter came up to me.

"Half a pint of the usual, young Mr. Jones?"

I smiled cheerfully and felt quite flattered to be known to the waiter (I suppose Mr. Jenkins had told him my name), and enrolled in the company of the Horse Boy to the extent of having a "usual."

Remembering my unfortunate experience, I declined; and the waiter, grinning more broadly than ever, remarked:

"Ah yes. We was a little under the weather last night."

"Under the table, you mean," I said.

"Oh that's very good!" said the waiter. "I must remember to tell that around!"

Although I hadn't meant it to be funny, I laughed as if I had, and looked forward to the prospect of being famous for it.

"Mr. R.'s been and gone," said the waiter. "You just missed

him." He looked down pointedly at the Horse Boy's tray. There was a little heap of messages and right on top was a folded paper addressed to "W.J."

Eagerly I went to pick it up.

"You got to stroke Jimmy's head first," said the waiter, restraining me. "All the gentlemen does. Custom of the 'ouse; and it's for luck, too."

"Of course," I said. "I forgot."

I felt grateful to be guided so agreeably in the ways of the London world; and I looked round, thinking how I might boast of it all when I got home.

The Horse Boy's head proved surprisingly cold, as if it was wet. The waiter sniggered. I glanced at my hand. It was shiny and black with something like printer's ink.

"No call to be angry, young Mr. Jones!" said the waiter, wiping off the remains of the ink from the Horse Boy's head with his napkin. "New gentlemen always has it done to 'em!"

I tried hard to take the stupid joke in good part. I reached to get my message; but the waiter gave it to me to prevent my dirtying all the others.

"There you go!" he said cheerfully. "We knew you'd do that!"

"What?"

"Push your hair back like that! You're always doing it, ain't you!"

It was a habit I never really knew I had. After all, habits are those things about you that only other people notice. The waiter, grinning very broadly, made me look in a mirror. There were two long black finger marks on my forehead. I tried to wipe them off with my sleeve.

"Don't do that, young Mr. Jones! You'll only make it worse. Just leave it and everybody'll know you're a regular of the Horse Boy. And that's nothing to be ashamed of!"

As all the customers were staring at me and laughing and grinning, I thought I'd better do the same, although I didn't feel like it.

The waiter nodded, approving my good humor, and said:

"Now you're a real Horse Boy, young Mr. Jones!"

"Only in parts," I said, pointing to my forehead.

"Oh that's a good one! I must remember to tell that one around!"

I read my message. It was very short.

"J.D. in the Sun in Splendour. Coalman's Alley. Blackfriars. After dark." It was signed: "Affectionately, R."

I showed it to the waiter. He gave me directions and said it was about twenty minutes' walk. I put a sixpence in the Horse Boy's tray and set off to meet John Diamond.

After dark. Blackfriars. Coalman's Alley. The Sun in Splendour! What a conjugation from gloom to glory! What a piling up of shades and shadows, of shrinking streets, unseen corners, wrong turnings and alleys as blind as bats . . . until the Sun in Splendour!

It hung over an open doorway, a little tarnished ball in spikes. There were a few steps leading down, and a smoky yellow glimmer coming up, as if the sun had had a misfortune and fallen downstairs, and was limping back up, one step at a time.

I went down with my heart and mind full of John Diamond. I pictured him sitting at a table next to Mr. Robinson: a needy, nervous person, who'd start and turn to Mr. Robinson for his nod and smile of, "Yes. That's him." Then he'd get up and come quickly towards me.

"I'm John Diamond!" he'd say; and we'd shake hands and there'd be an instant warmth between us.

But it wasn't at all like that.

The parlor was crowded and noisy; and the only thing that came to greet me was a vicious-looking black dog, which, however, changed its mind about biting me when it sniffed at my coat.

I suppose my clothes still had some country smells about them that reminded the dog of the open air and fields; for it wouldn't leave me alone and kept pushing its nose into me and turning round to the parlor as if to say: "I told you so! I told you all along that there *was* a countryside! Come and have a smell!"

I tried to push it away, as its affection for what I was wearing was attracting a good deal of interest; and, I can tell you, it wasn't at all like the interest Mrs. Carwardine had displayed. It was savage and envious; it was inquisitive and crafty; it made me thrust my hands into my pockets, to make sure they were still there, and look about for a corner where I could hide.

I hunched up my shoulders and tried to look as if my fine clothes were not my own, but that I'd just murdered William Jones for them, and was therefore a perfectly ordinary boy, not worth a second glance.

The parlor of the Sun in Splendour was a dreadful, smoky, stinking hole of a place, lit by two huge black lanterns that were chained to the ceiling as if to stop them being stolen away.

I couldn't see Mr. Robinson anywhere; and without him, I'd no hope at all of finding John Diamond. For all I knew, he might have been sitting there already, glancing at me and wondering if the nervous, out-of-place–looking boy was David Jones's son.

Every face I looked at might easily have been John Diamond's. They all looked needy, furtive, restless and anxious to be out of the light. I felt a touch on my sleeve. I looked down. A great hulk of a man, with something like a dead cat on his head, had pushed along his bench and precipitated someone off it at the other end, and was indicating that I might sit on the scrap of seat he'd thus provided.

Not wanting to offend him, I did so, and the black dog settled down to gnaw at my shoes.

"Stranger?" inquired the man.

I told him I was looking for a Mr. John Diamond.

"I didn't ask thee what tha' was looking for. I asked if tha' was a stranger."

I admitted that I was.

"What's tha' sup then? What's tha' booze, tha' drink? Gin? Brandy? Ale?"

Remembering the sherry, I said I was partial to mild ale. Instantly he shouted for the landlord and a pint of ale was put before me, for which my new friend paid.

He was off a ship, he told me, a Newcastle collier, and was a stranger himself. He thought all strangers ought to stick together; that way, they wouldn't feel strange.

I think he'd had a good deal to drink; but he wasn't the worse for it, rather the better, in fact. Most likely, he was a real terror when he was sober.

I tried to buy him a drink, but he wouldn't hear of it as he'd just been paid off and was in "foonds." I was quite sorry when he got up to go.

Several other men went soon after, and so did the dog. I heard it barking, and the sounds of an argument outside in the street. Then the dog came back eating something. By its pleased expression, it was probably a finger.

The parlor was half empty now, and I was alone at the table. I took out my watch to see the time. Instantly I felt a staring of eyes upon my back and a sensation of cobwebby hands in my pockets. The very air seemed to be composed of invisible thieves. I put the watch away without even looking at it.

There was a little crowd of boys round a table on the other side of the parlor. They were watching me intently. Suddenly, and with a horrible shock, I saw that one of them was the savage boy that Mr. Seed had caught! I went cold as I remembered his warning: "Run for your life!"

But he made no move towards me; he didn't even seem to recognize me. I sat still and wondered at the coincidence of his being there. Then the thought flashed upon my mind that *he* was John Diamond!

That's why he was there! I remembered that the dwarf had caught him soon after I'd heard Mr. Robinson whistling. Mr. Robinson must have sent him and the dwarf had made a terrible mistake!

As I looked at him—wild and savage creature that he was!—I couldn't help sweating as I recalled my ideas of taking John Diamond home and even going to school with him. The prospect was quite staggering. My Uncle Turner would probably have him shot.

One of the boys—not him—stood up and walked over to my table.

He looked at me carefully and then said:

"You got a dirty face, mister." He pointed to his own forehead, which was by no means above reproach. "There."

"I know," I said. "I got it in the Horse Boy."

The boy grinned; at first I thought rather menacingly, but afterwards I discovered it was only the shape of his mouth. When he wanted to be menacing, he looked quite different. He was, I supposed, offering me friendship, as from one boy to another, in a world of men.

"Come along over an' sit wiv' us," he said. "You ken buy us a drink if you like."

I looked at his table and saw a good many reasons for not going there. Eight, in fact; and they were all watching me. But I thought the boy might turn unpleasant if I refused; and besides, I was anxious to talk to the savage one.

"Be pleased to," I said; and walked back with him.

I sat as near as I could to the one I thought might be John Diamond. I thought he might be a year or so older than me, as he was oddly wrinkled. As soon as I could, I asked him his name.

He answered me exactly as he'd answered Mr. Seed. He spat at me.

"He ain't much of a talker," said the boy who'd fetched me over. "He allus does that."

"What's his name, then?"

"Dunno. We calls him Shot-in-the-'ead."

"Why?"

"Dunno. I'll 'ave gin. And me friends likewise."

The landlord, not trusting them with private receptacles, brought a jug.

"That's a 'andsome purse," said one, when I paid.

"It—it's real Morocco leather," I said; and then, not wanting to seem too rich, I added, "My grandma gave it to me."

" 'Is gran'ma! Cor! That's 'is muvver's muvver!"

"No it ain't! It's 'is pa's!"

"Go on! Tell us!"

"It's my—my mother's mother."

"Get that! Get that! It's 'is muTHer's muTHer!"

"Did she give yer that coat an' weskit, too?"

"N-no! My f-father—"

"Cor! 'Is fa-a-ather! 'E's got a fa-a-ather, too!"

"No—no!" I said, anxious to disclaim any further possessions. "He's dead! Honest, he is!"

"Oh! There now! What d'yer know! 'Is fa-a-ather's gone an' deaded 'isself!"

They were leaning across the table and beginning to pull at my coat and shirt. Also the dog had come back and was showing an equal interest in my shoes.

I was very frightened. The mood had changed so quickly that I didn't know what to do. Although I was not exactly a stranger to warfare, and had, on occasion, been referred to as "a disgusting little ruffian," there were eight boys against me and they could easily have killed me.

The first boy was now demonstrating how he looked when he really wanted to be menacing; and was making a very creditable job of it.

Suddenly I thought I had seen him before. I *had* seen him before! I had seen all of them. They were the ragged boys who had attacked the dwarf's house!

Shot-in-the-Head—or whatever his name was—was no more

John Diamond than he was Lord Mayor of London! He'd been outside the house just as Mr. Seed said: trying to burn it down!

I stood up and got hold of the jug, meaning to hit out with it. The landlord came and took it away.

"I won't 'ave no wiolence in 'ere," he grunted. "Not from the likes of you."

He departed. I don't know where to. To hell, I hoped.

I clenched my fists and offered, rather hopelessly, to fight my opponents one at a time. I thought they might respect me for it.

They didn't. They declined my offer on the grounds that they didn't like my face, or the way I talked, and that they were going to alter both. Or words to that effect.

I began to back away towards the steps. I remember very clearly that the dog followed and was snarling and whining in a peculiar way. I think he could smell how frightened I was.

I felt the first step behind me. I turned. Shot-in-the-Head was standing in my way. I looked straight into his eyes, trying desperately to remind him of how I'd let *him* go. It was his turn now.

His eyes were wild and utterly pitiless. The dwarf had been right. He would have killed me and never thought twice about it.

The expression "selling my life dearly" came into my head. On rapid reflection I decided I would sooner try to buy it. I threw my purse at the crowd, punched Shot-in-the-Head in the face, and fled up into the street!

It was only when I was outside and had run about twenty yards, and was congratulating myself on the brilliance of my escape, that I realized that I would have been better off if I'd stayed where I was.

In the parlor I might have been badly kicked and punched and probably bitten; but no one would have dared to do more than that. They wouldn't have killed me with people about. Out in the street however, in dark, empty Coalman's Alley, it was different.

They came up out of the Sun in Splendour like quick black rats. I caught a glimpse of knives and a fearful-looking iron hook that would have ripped open an ox.

My purse hadn't stopped them. They weren't mercenary. It was me they wanted, not my money. I know people are always saying that it's better to be wanted for yourself alone rather than for your possessions; but not when it's your blood they want, all over the street.

Perhaps, if I'd had that six months with my Uncle Turner and been made a man of, I'd have turned with my back to the wall and fought off my enemies until they lay in a groaning heap at my feet.

As it was, I shrieked for help and ran like mad, without caring what anybody thought of me, until I fell over a loose cobble at the end of Coalman's Alley.

I thought I was done for. I lay, shaking with terror and hoping I'd be taken for dead. Something began tugging and gnawing at my foot. It was the dog. I was going to kick it, when I remembered that a dead boy wouldn't.

Suddenly I realized that nothing had happened. The noise of pursuit had stopped. I could hear somebody whistling.

> *"I care for nobody, no, not I;*
> *And nobody cares for me!"*

It was Mr. Robinson and Mr. Jenkins, on their way to meet me in the Sun in Splendour. My pursuers must have seen them and taken fright.

Mr. Robinson helped me up. He was rather angry.

"Why didn't you wait inside the parlor, young Jones?"

I tried to explain what had happened.

"Spoilin' for a fight, were you, young feller-me-lad?" said Mr. Jenkins.

"I didn't start it."

"That's what they all say!"

"We'd better go and see if John Diamond has turned up yet," said Mr. Robinson.

"He wasn't there!" I said quickly.

"How do you know? You've never clapped eyes on him."

"I—I didn't see anybody waiting," I said.

I was very unwilling to go back along Coalman's Alley. Although the murderous boys had vanished, I felt very strongly that they had merely lifted, like the London fog, and were hovering, waiting to come back. Every shadow seemed to hold them; and every breath of foul air seemed to whisper: "We'll get you! Just you wait and see!"

"You were a fool, young Jones," said Mr. Robinson. "I went to a lot of trouble to find John Diamond for you. For your sake, I hope he wasn't there; because at the first sign of trouble, he'd have gone for good."

We went back into the Sun in Splendour. Mr. Robinson looked quickly round the parlor.

"Well, he's not here now."

"Shall we wait?" suggested Mr. Jenkins.

Mr. Robinson went over to a table next to where the boys had been sitting. There was a piece of white pasteboard on the floor. He picked it up and brought it back. He showed it to Mr. Jenkins and then to me. It was a trade card. It said:

"John Diamond. General Agent and Guide. Discretion Guaranteed."

He *had* been in the parlor. And he had gone.

12

THIS WAS A GREAT blow. I stared at the trade card, biting my lip and, I've no doubt, pushing back my hair as if to let a little air into my brain.

John Diamond had been sitting there all the time, and I'd missed him! I felt angry and guilty and humiliated and very *provincial* over the whole affair. If only I hadn't been so sure that John Diamond was a boy, because *I* was a boy, and jumped to the conclusion that he was Shot-in-the-Head, then I might have looked round at the grown men and not got into that fight.

I say, I *might*; but I couldn't get rid of a feeling that, somehow, I'd been tricked and that the boys had deliberately prevented me from meeting John Diamond.

My fury against them, and myself, rose considerably, and wasn't in the least helped by Mr. Jenkins remarking that I should have kept my eyes open and not indulged myself in the boyish pleasure of fighting with other boys like a pack of dogs.

By the way he said it, it was plain that he thought I was nothing more than a stupid country oaf who hadn't been able to take a little teasing from a few poor London boys without flying into a rage.

I'm sure he thought that everybody in the country, when they weren't chewing straw, went about sticking pitchforks into each other and setting fire to hayricks.

I informed him, as calmly as I could, exactly what I thought of London and its boys, *and* the filthy place I'd been brought to, which, as a country person, I wouldn't even have kept pigs in.

Here the landlord came up rather threateningly and said I was a troublemaker and he knew my sort and I'd better get out if I knew what was good for me.

Hastily Mr. Robinson and Mr. Jenkins bundled me up the steps and outside, as if they were frightened that I would commit some fresh act of country outrage and they'd have to pay.

For a moment, I thought they were going to wash their hands of me, and leave me in Coalman's Alley. I thought of the poor London boys, waiting in dark corners, to come out and tease me . . . with knives and that great iron hook.

"I'm sorry," I said, looking hopefully at Mr. Robinson. "I'm truly sorry to—to have caused you any inconvenience, sir."

Mr. Robinson leaned back against the wall and stuck his thumbs in his waistcoat pockets. He sighed.

"Ah well! We were all young once!"

"Speak for yourself," said Mr. Jenkins solemnly. "*I* was never young! Born with a quill be'ind me ear, like a little goslin', I was!"

At once this had the effect of lightening everybody's mood; and I couldn't help laughing at Mr. Jenkins's mournful face as he lamented his premature entry into manhood.

"Ah youth!" he sighed. "I got an action for damages against the loss of it; with costs awarded in favor of my 'eart."

"Ah youth!" echoed Mr. Robinson. "The season of hope and delight!"

"Ah youth!" I said, feeling that a contribution was expected of me; but got no further as I couldn't think of anything that made it a peculiarly desirable state to be in.

Suddenly Mr. Robinson jumped into activity.

"Come along!" he said. "Let's go and find John Diamond! He's sure to be at the Cock and Fountain!"

We linked arms—me in the middle—and set off down Coalman's Alley: three of the cheerfullest people in the world. I think we sang; I'm sure we whistled, as we marched through the night in pursuit of John Diamond.

Always linked together, we never parted once. Never apart, lifting our arms over posts, twisting sideways down narrow alleys and butting our way round St. Paul's churchyard. Never apart, running up steps and down steps, and tramping through courts and round grave squares. Never apart, no matter what inconvenience we caused.

"Beg pardon, ma'am, but we've got a country lad here and can't let him go!"

"Beg pardon, sir, but this boy's been took sick!"

"Excuse us! Excuse us, but we've got one of the princes in the Tower!"

"Out of the way! Out of the way! Mad boy! Mad boy! Beware!"

Mr. Jenkins, the lawyer, kept calling me his little Habeas Corpus, and his rosy-faced Assumpsit. Mr. Robinson said that Mr. Jenkins was a low fellow to use such language in the street. Mr. Jenkins appealed to me that Mr. Robinson was jeering at him for having a mother in " 'Oundsditch." Mr. Robinson said I should ignore a person who dropped his aitches.

"My haitches may be in default," said Mr. Jenkins solemnly. "But my 'eart is in the right place." And he thumped himself on the chest.

It was a wonderful night; or at least, that part of it was. There was a fine rain falling, that made the stones shine and doubled the houses and street-lamps; and sent everyone hurrying deep in their coats, with watery noses and eyes.

We searched for John Diamond high, we searched for him low; and we searched in those middle places where people played at cards and looked at you when you came in, as if it was your turn to deal.

John Diamond wasn't in the Cock and Fountain; and he'd just left the Magpie and Stump. He'd been in the Goose and Gridiron half an hour earlier; and in and out of the Swan and Cap like a dose of salts. His chair in the Elephant and Castle was still warm; and we saw the place where he'd just been standing, inside the door of the Harrow and Lamb.

I wondered if John Diamond knew that we were after him, and was purposely leading us such a dance, through a night of a thousand gaudy painted animals, groaning and squealing on rusty hinges, high in the dark running air. I don't know how many Red Lions, and Black Lions, and White Lions we saw, banging and snapping as if, at that very moment, they had gobbled up John Diamond whole, and left only an empty chair behind.

Empty chairs, empty places and once, an empty glass. What a shadowy, ghostly figure he was. Did he exist, even? *Was* there a John Diamond? There was nothing to prove it but a trade card, and places where he'd been. What did he look like? Was he tall? Was he dark or fair? I asked.

"Ordinary enough. You wouldn't look twice if you didn't know."

"Didn't know what?"

"Why, that he was John Diamond, of course! Let's try the Eagle and Child!"

A crying baby in the talons of the worst bird I ever saw. As I looked up at the sign, I thought that the baby must have been a country child, as the eagle was a real Londoner, from its corkscrew tail to the tip of its iron hooked beak.

Again the empty chair. How long ago? Mr. Robinson held up his fingers. Five minutes. His gray gloves were streaked and darkened from the rain, and there was a large bump to show where his seal ring was. His hand looked like a spider with a frightfully injured leg.

We stood outside, leaning against the wall. The rain was still coming down and making little silver hedgehogs in the puddles between the stones.

"I'm done!" said Mr. Jenkins. "I've 'ad enough. It's past midnight and me ma will be worryin'."

"She knows you're in good company," said Mr. Robinson, examining both sides of his spider hand.

Mr. Jenkins shook his head and turned to me.

"Listen, young feller-me-lad. We've turned the town over for you. Now there's no hard feelin's. No 'ard feelin's, is there, Robinson, old man?"

"No hard feelings, Jenkins."

"You're sure of that?" asked Mr. Jenkins, with a sudden twinge of anxiety.

"Oh yes."

"All right, then. Now you tell me, young feller-me-lad, just what it is you want with John Diamond. Come on! Out with it!"

Suddenly, all the good humor had gone from his face. It was as keen and sharp as the eagle's, over his head.

In an instant, the night had changed; not the weather, but the feeling of it. It was quiet, tense and, I thought, dangerous. On one side of me was Mr. Robinson, still examining his glove. On the other was Mr. Jenkins, who wore no gloves and had bitten finger-nails.

I'd always thought that Mr. Robinson had been the superior one, and that Mr. Jenkins had been the weaker character, only do-ing what he'd been told. But now it was Mr. Jenkins who had his hand on my shoulder and gripping hard.

"It's something about that ten thousand pound, ain't it! That's what it is!"

He shook me.

"Come on! Tell us!"

"Let me go!" I muttered.

I was not very frightened of Mr. Jenkins. He was rather thin and unhealthy-looking; and I could see that Mr. Robinson was not taking his part.

"It's in Seed's house, ain't it!" he went on, still shaking.

"Why—why should it be there?"

"Ah! So you *do* know about it! Old Seed's sittin' on it!"

"Why?"

"Don't you know? That's where your pa and John Diamond's late lamented first set up in business. It's under a floorboard, ain't it! And you know which one!"

"I don't know—I don't know!"

"Come on, or I'll—"

"That's enough, Jenkins," said Mr. Robinson, at last taking an interest. "If young Jones says he doesn't know, he doesn't. He's a truthful lad. That's something you lawyers don't understand. All he wants is John Diamond. He don't want you; he don't want me. It's all to be for old John."

He pushed Mr. Jenkins's hand off my shoulder and put his arm around it, quite affectionately.

"Now do you see what you've done!" he said, in mock reproach. "You've sent poor old Jenkins off his head. That ten thousand pounds he's so mad about, was all dead and buried before you came along. It was old history; twenty years old. But as soon as you appeared, it all came back to life. Ain't you ashamed to have woken it up?"

"And that ain't the only thing," said Mr. Jenkins darkly.

I don't know what Mr. Jenkins meant by that; but it was something that made Mr. Robinson very angry. He looked at him sharply; and Mr. Jenkins looked away.

"Let's go."

"Where to?" said Mr. Jenkins.

"To see John Diamond."

"Where this time? The Goat and Compasses?"

"No. You know where."

"I'm not goin'."

Until that moment, I'd given up all hope of there being such a person as John Diamond; but suddenly I knew that he existed, and that I was going to meet him.

Mr. Jenkins went off, complaining bitterly, and Mr. Robinson took my arm. We began to walk; and, although the streets were quite empty, I had a feeling that we were being followed. I wondered if it could be that John Diamond, Agent, Guide, Discretion Guaranteed, was now pursuing us?

We walked down a steepish hill at the bottom of which I could see a thick gray blanket of mist. It was threadbare in patches and showed glints of black water. It was the river.

Presently the road began to mount again. It grew broader and there were parapets on either side.

"This is London Bridge," said Mr. Robinson, in an oddly practiced sort of way. "There used to be houses on it; but they took them down as they weren't safe. It's a very old bridge and they reckon that fifty watermen a year are drowned trying to shoot the arches. If you listen, you can hear the water rushing through."

I listened; and the water, although I couldn't see it because of the mist, made a fearsome noise, like a thousand snakes.

"Down that way," went on Mr. Robinson, pointing to the left, "lies Greenwich and Deptford. If you strain your eyes, you can see the masts of ships."

I looked and saw a sprinkling of thin spires and poles sticking up out of the mist like a giant's pincushion. Below, unseen lanterns made cloudy yellow eyes.

"Is—is he on a ship?"

"They say," said Mr. Robinson, crossing the street and walking on the right-hand side of the bridge, "that the bridge is haunted. They say it's haunted by the spirits of children. They buried children, you know, in the foundations. They buried them alive. For luck."

He stopped and leaned over the parapet.

"Where is he, Mr. Robinson? Where is John Diamond?"

"On the bridge."

I looked. The bridge gleamed and vanished, like a broad smile, among dark houses on the other side. There was nobody on it.

"I—I can't see him."

"He's leaning over the parapet."

"He's—"

"My card, William Jones. My card, sir."

Mr. Robinson fumbled in his waistcoat pocket and handed me a piece of pasteboard. It read:

"John Diamond. General Agent and Guide. Discretion Guaranteed."

"Like it says," murmured John Diamond, looking intently down into the mists. "Discretion guaranteed."

13

DISCRETION GUARANTEED. I never was in a more discreet place in all my life.

A wind came in gusts, driving the fine rain straight across the bridge and leaving it swept cold, gleaming and empty. There was a moon, of sorts, rolling through the muddy air like an old drowned eye.

John Diamond remained staring down into the river so that I

could only make out the edge of his face, which was whitened by the moon. I think he must have had eyes in the back of his head, for he said:

"Didn't they teach you any manners, William? Didn't they tell you it's rude to stand and stare, with your mouth open, like a fish? Weren't you taught to say, 'Pleased to meet you' when you're introduced? Your father would have known that. My father always said that David Jones was the best-mannered man he'd ever met."

"Pleased to meet you," I muttered obediently; and tried to get over my astonishment and to understand why he had hidden himself in Mr. Robinson, why he had been running all over the town in pursuit of himself, and why he'd brought me to this grim, deserted place.

A clock began to chime the half hour; then another, and another, further and further away, as if they were all lost in the dark and were crying: "Where—are—you? Where—are—you? *I'm*—here . . . *I'm* here . . ."

"There are," said John Diamond, "one hundred and five churches with peals of bells, many of which were recast from the bells that were melted down in The Great Fire. If you look back, you can see the Monument, put up by Sir Christopher Wren to mark where the fire began, in Pudding Lane."

If he'd stood on his head, he couldn't have bewildered me more.

"You ought to be paying me for all this, William," he said mildly. "It's how I get my living, you know. I show strangers round the town and point out interesting items. Jenkins puts them on to me. Well-to-do young men from the country, like yourself. I show them the high life, I show them the low life; and I show them where they can play cards. Then I show them where they can borrow money to pay their debts, and where they can buy pistols to blow their brains out when they're ruined."

Although he didn't say any of this bitterly, it was plain he thought his work was degrading. Stupidly, I said:

"I'm sorry." And of course he took it in the wrong way.

"Who for? The young gentlemen?"

"No—no! I didn't mean that."

"Oh! I see! You're sorry for me. You think how terrible it must be for the son of your father's old partner to have sunk so low. Well, you shouldn't think that. I haven't sunk at all. In fact, you might say that I've climbed. I never knew any better, you see. My late lamented—as Jenkins would call him—*lost everything*, so to speak, before I had a chance to get used to it. I only heard stories of wealth; I never actually knew it."

By the way he'd said, "lost everything," and hunched his shoulders at the same time, I guessed that he knew everything about how my father had cheated his. But it didn't seem to worry him; indeed, by his unchanging attitude of leaning over the parapet towards where the water rushed underneath, that it was all, all water under the bridge.

Perhaps I ought to have remembered that fifty watermen a year were drowned as that water went under the bridge; but I didn't. All I could think about was that the thin, negligent figure before me was John Diamond and that maybe the ghost of his father and the ghost of mine were also standing on the bridge, and watching this meeting of their sons.

"What was it you wanted to see me about, William? Be quick, or we'll *both* catch our deaths of cold!"

Perhaps I should have noted the emphasis on "*both*," as if "one" would merely have been unfortunate and not a disaster.

"Was it about that ten thousand pounds, William?"

How I wished it had have been! How I wished I could have brought *something* for John Diamond! I felt so deeply sad and sorry for him, standing there and being proud and dignified over his father's ruin. I wanted to do everything for him; but I could do nothing. I wanted to promise him that I would make up everything to him, just as soon as I came into my money. In short, my heart was very full, at that moment, of the best feelings I'd ever had; and it was with real misery that I told him that I knew nothing at all about the ten thousand pounds.

"I thought not," he said. "Jenkins was sure that you did; but he's money mad. Doesn't appreciate the finer feelings. No breeding, really. He thought you were telling lies. Lawyers and their clerks tell so many lies that they always think everybody else is lying. But I knew that you were telling the truth. So tell me why you wanted to see me?"

I told him. I told him as warmly and energetically as I could, about my father's remorse and about his restless ghost; and that all I wanted was to set the past wrong right . . . somehow, anyhow, even if I could only do it with the strength of my feelings . . .

He listened, occasionally shaking his head, as if in sympathy, and shifting from one foot to another. I remember thinking how easy it was when you opened your heart, and that the worst only happened when you hid things.

"I knew it was just feelings," he said when I'd finished. "I knew it all the time. I knew there wasn't anything clever in it. You're not very clever, are you, William? And that's surprising, considering that you're David Jones's son. *He* was clever. You should have heard my late lamented talking about him! Clever as a cartload of monkeys, was old David Jones! But he didn't pass it on. All you inherited was the money; and guilt. Well, as they say, a fool and his money are soon parted. But the guilt goes on."

For the first time he looked at me. He turned his face and looked over his shoulder. I saw, with the most horrible sick feeling, that he hated me.

Even as I had inherited guilt from my father, he had inherited hatred from his.

He was eaten up with it; he was mad with it. He had nursed it in his heart for twenty years. He had dreamed about it as a child; he'd planned and schemed what he'd do if ever he found David Jones or anyone belonging to him.

All this he told me as we stood on the bridge, with the water rushing beneath and the wind driving across, so that half his words were lost. His face was wet with rain, and it looked like tears.

There was nothing I could say or do, because he knew that he was in the right and his hatred was justified. That was the worst part about it—his being in the right, I mean. He hated me because of what one dead man had done to another, so there was no way out of it.

Suddenly he stopped talking; and I thought that was the end. I started to walk away from him, filled with deepest gloom and despair; when I heard him whistling. It was his old tune and peculiarly piercing. In spite of the wind, I think it must have drifted down to Greenwich.

> *"I care for nobody, no, not I;*
> *And nobody cares for me!"*

Even as I looked, I saw, creeping up onto the bridge and coming towards me, like the ghosts of all the murdered children hell-bent on revenge, the London boys with their knives and the great iron hook! He had whistled them up!

14

WHEN YOU ARE KILLED, suddenly and violently, I always supposed that there would be a moment—a tiny moment—when your soul rushed out of your body at a great speed, and left it behind like a falling towel.

I felt that, if I looked back, I would have seen William Jones, lying by the parapet of London Bridge, all mangled and bloody, like Julius Caesar.

I expected at any moment that I would become transparent, and be grasped by the ear and taken off by whichever party had the chief claim . . . I mean angels or devils.

I felt I must have been killed, else how was it that I was running like the wind, with no worse injury than a ripped sleeve that had happened as I'd gone too close to a knife?

I had run straight at the boys instead of away from them; and they, who had been ready to fly after me, had been taken by surprise.

I ran, I suppose, just as a fox might have run; and, at the same time, uttered a shriek which, as they say, would have struck terror into the boldest heart. Anyway, it struck terror into mine. I'd never heard such a shriek; and, when I realized it had come from me, I felt unnatural.

I had a sensation of the boys, or one of them, at least, melting away before me; and then I was pounding along the bridge and back into the town.

The only safety I knew, was in the dwarf's house in Hanging Sword Alley. As far as I remembered, it lay to the west of St. Paul's Cathedral and near to the river.

They were both large articles—St. Paul's and the River Thames —and, you would think, not easily missed. But I promise you that as soon as I left the bridge, they both vanished utterly from the face of the earth.

I never saw the river again though I twisted and turned a thousand times, and went down every sloping alley and every crazy winding street; and the great cathedral came up and peeped over the housetops only for seconds, as if it was playing at some huge and lumbering hide-and-seek. Now it was this side of me; now it was that; and God alone knew which was east and which was west; and I cursed Sir Christopher Wren for neglecting to paint on his dome which of its many sides was the one I had seen from the house of Mr. Seed.

I did not think much about John Diamond as I ran, any more than a rabbit, I suppose, thinks about the man in the moon when he's bolting like mad from the dogs.

I could think only about the private hailstorm of footsteps that followed me wherever I went: now gaining, now scattering, now seeming to run invisibly by my side.

It was a terrible sound; and even now, when I hear hail beating down on a roof, my heart thunders as I remember that merciless pursuit. I cannot even walk down a passage by night, without seeing again—as I saw a hundred times—a grim little figure come out of nowhere, whistle, and creep towards me.

They were whistling to each other all the time: fierce little noises like pins and needles in the night.

At first I thought they were hunting cries—whistles instead of horns. I never guessed, until it was too late, that they were signals, from one hunter to another, as they drove me deeper and deeper into town.

I thought it was just bad luck that I never reached an open street where I might have got help; and I thought it was just marvelous good luck that, whenever I seemed to be cut off, there was always one last alleyway that appeared mysteriously and offered me an escape.

Sometimes upstairs windows opened and people shouted down for the dreadful clatter to stop; and I panted, "Save me! Save me!" and then wept and swore when the windows banged shut.

If ever I learned anything during that night, it was that, if you should hear the noise of running feet, you should not be angry, but think that somebody down below might be gasping and groaning and struggling on to save his life. If you should see a boy raise his fists as if to bang on your door and then stumble away, it is not because he's a dirty little ruffian, but because he's just caught sight of somebody coming round a corner with a terrible hook.

I stopped. Not because I was tired—I could have run another yard, I think—but because the hailstorm behind me had stopped. This was the worst moment. The sudden stoppage of footsteps has always been a particular nightmare of mine.

I leaned against a wall, listening. I could hear nothing, absolutely nothing. I knew the boys were close, but I did not know where.

I was in a stony passageway, between tall, toppling tenements that went up so high that even the moonlight only got halfway down, before giving up the ghost on the dirty walls.

Only the rain came down. It was falling in large, sullen drops. I looked up and saw a line of washing stretched across the narrow sky like hanged men in a row, sullenly weeping rain.

I thought I might cry out, just once more, for help. I would shriek, "Save me! Please save me!"

But I couldn't. There was something over my mouth. It smelled foul and tasted bitter. It was a hand!

At the same time another hand pushed me violently against the wall, which seemed to open and engulf me. It was a door and it shut as soon as I was inside.

I think my blood would have run cold, if any part of me had still been able to run. But, like the rest of me, it was quite worn out. I stood, in total blackness, with a vague sensation that I had been put aside, like a leg of lamb, to be eaten later.

Outside I heard the whistles start up again, and the scattering of hail. It went on for I don't know how long; but no one came into my darkness.

At last the hail dwindled away and all I could hear, apart from the grunting and creaking of the building over my head, was the ticking of my father's watch. It seemed quite undisturbed.

I began to feel about for the door when it opened in quite an unexpected place. Then it shut again and I was no longer alone. I knew that by the sound of breathing, other than my own.

"Who are you?"

The hand, as before, was put over my mouth. I was not to speak. I didn't really mind, as I didn't have much to say.

I felt myself begin to be pulled through the darkness. I followed without offering the smallest resistance. I was too tired.

I stumbled against the beginning of some stairs. At once I was gripped sharply round the wrist. Nails dug into me. I was to be quiet. I followed up the stairs, waving each foot cautiously before putting it down.

I think there were a hundred stairs and about the same number of landings. I began to see dimly, as we rose, doors and doors, and heaps of rubbish, some of which looked like dead men.

I thought one of them stirred; and all about I began to hear vague stirrings, and murmurings, and sighings, and once, the small cry of a baby that made me jump with alarm.

I thought we must be pretty near hell by now, although we'd been going the wrong way. I don't think I would have been very surprised to have seen Satan come out of one of the doors, and welcome me inside, and thank the dark, hunched-up figure that was leading me, for his trouble and care.

I stumbled again; and received a fierce pinch. We came at last to a ladder, propped up against a wall. I groaned quietly at the thought of climbing still further; and was kicked for it.

The figure began to mount the ladder, and I followed. The wood was slimy to the touch.

I looked up and saw that a slice of the night was appearing and enlarging itself into a square. The rain came down and the sky was blotted out for a moment as the figure obscured it. Then the figure was gone, leaving only a beckoning hand behind.

I took it and climbed up into the open night. We were on the roof. Or, rather, we were standing on a narrow pathway between two roofs that rose on either side like steep little hills.

One end of the pathway was covered over by what looked like a pile of old coats. It made another little house, balancing on the first one, like the crazy top of a house of cards. Within, I could make out a faint glimmering of coals. My guide pointed.

"Git inside," he muttered. "It's where I dosses. You ken doss there, too."

My guide was Shot-in-the-Head; and he urged me forward, towards his place of residence, with every appearance of pride.

15

I WOKE UP to a bright sky and a view of my Uncle Turner and two fat beadles in a row. They were standing on a short stretch of wall and smoking, to pass the time, while they waited to take me into custody. After a few moments, they resolved themselves into chimney pots, and I remembered where I was.

I was in Shot-in-the-Head's high residence and being heated all down one side by an iron basket half-filled with glowing coals. Shot-in-the-Head himself was nowhere to be seen, so I crawled outside to inspect the landscape.

My situation was distinctly airy. All around me chimney-stacks and pots of gigantic size loomed and leaned and scowled and puffed, and balanced themselves uncomfortably on the edges of slate hills, as if they'd decided there was no such thing as gravity and were going to prove it by jumping off.

I saw Shot-in-the-Head. He was crouching on top of a roof, with his chin in his fists and the wind blowing his rusty hair about. He was enjoying the morning sunshine.

He waved and slid down the slates to meet me.

"Yus," he said, looking at me rather sharply. "Yus."

His voice was harsh and hoarse, like an iron bolt that had seized up from not being used; but his eyes were as bright as if he'd just been polishing them.

I said: "Good morning."

"You 'it me," he said.

"I didn't!"

"Yus. In the Splenner."

For a moment I thought he was referring to some part of his anatomy, and I wondered where it could be; but then he opened his mouth and indicated that he'd recently lost a tooth, so I knew that he meant the Sun in Splendour where I'd punched him in the face.

I told him I'd only been trying to get away; and he told me that I'd been a right addle-cove not to have knowed that he'd been trying to help, as he'd knowed that they was only wanting to get me outside to chop me up as they couldn't wet their chives in the Splenner.

After that, he said, I'd fair give him kittings when he'd been penny-boying me back to his doss.

"What?" I said.

"Wot wot?" said he, scratching his head over my ignorance.

I gave up; but afterwards, when I got used to the way he talked, I realized that all the time I'd been running through the night, Shot-in-the-Head had been skillfully driving me, like a sheep to the slaughter; only it hadn't been to slaughter but to safety, on account of my having saved *him* from Mr. Seed.

Somehow it didn't seem right to thank him. I don't think he wanted to be thanked. He'd done what he'd done because he'd done it, and that was that, if you know what I mean.

He brought out some food: a piece of blackened meat (I don't know from what animal, or person, even), which he'd cooked himself, and a lump of bread.

While we ate he told me how he and his mates had knowed me by the black marks on my hands and face. He grinned and I felt all my old fear and bewilderment about John Diamond rising up again. Only this time it was ten times worse. I realized how cunningly he'd marked me out by the paint on the Horse Boy; and how well he must have known me to have done it. He had seen right through me all the time.

I thought at first that he'd called himself Robinson just for my benefit; but even Shot-in-the-Head knew him as Robinson, although he called him "Mr. Rob-a-Son," which, I suppose, was near enough. So I wondered what crime he had committed that made him hide John Diamond, except on his trade card.

Mr. Robinson was well-known to Shot-in-the-Head and his mates, particularly to Liverguts, who was the boy with the iron hook, and not to be trifled with.

It had been Mr. Robinson all the time who had been behind the attacks on the dwarf's house; and there were several others going on at the same time.

It was all business, really. If people wanted to get other people out of their dosses, they went to Mr. Robinson, who went to Liverguts and it was all fixed up.

"Yes," said Shot-in-the-Head. "Mr. Rob-a-Son wants you chopped." He stood up and went along the flat pathway from his house and leaned over a low parapet at the end. He pointed down into the deep slit of the street.

"You keep up 'ere," he said. "Dahn there you'll git chopped as soon as spit." He spat; and it was very quick.

"How long for?"

"Dunno. Long as yer likes."

He looked at me wonderingly, as if he couldn't understand why I should ever want to leave.

"Ah!" he said suddenly. "Yus. If yer wants to go somewhere, I gin'rally goes be'ind them pots."

He looked very mysterious and I guessed that he meant the privy and was informing me, as delicately as he could, that every convenience was to hand. He himself, I noticed, used a broken-off pot two roofs away and watered right down into it. He told me he did this because he had a grudge against the people who lived in the house, and was trying to put their fire out.

"Got to go," he said. "You keep 'ere."

"Where are you going?"

"Wiv me mates, on the snick-an-lurk."

"What's that?"

"Wot's wot?"

"Snick-an-lurk."

He scratched his head. He didn't know another word for it. Then he said, "Yus."

He reached across me, put his hand into my waistcoat pocket, took out my watch and put it in his own pocket. Then he returned the watch and said:

"Snick-an-lurk. See?"

I saw.

He looked hard at my waistcoat and then beckoned me inside his house. It was warm and smoky and roofed over with wooden planks. The back and sides consisted entirely of ancient coats and gowns and waistcoats and jackets and pairs of breeches that hung down like bell-pulls.

It was such a venerable feast of ripe old clothing that, once inside, you felt like a moth at its birthday party, wondering where to begin.

Shot-in-the-Head began diving his hand into the walls, where it kept vanishing, sometimes up to the elbow, in the hundreds of pockets that served him for cupboards and drawers.

He brought out his treasures. He had watches—better than mine—brooches, rings, a snuffbox, dozens of gilt buttons and buckles, and the top part of a plated candlestick. I never saw any coins; but I don't think he needed them as I'm sure he never paid for anything in his life.

He wasn't so much a thief as a magpie; he just liked things that shone. I often wondered why he didn't nick my watch; but I suppose that, as long as it was in a pocket under his roof, it was all the same.

He must have had hundreds of pounds worth of goods in his house; but it was only the glitter that pleased him. The strangest thing I ever saw was on one morning when Shot-in-the-Head was crouching on his roof and staring intently and enviously towards a particular object in the east. It was the gold cross on the top of St. Paul's. He wanted it, I think.

He put away his property, told me to keep the fire going (there was a heap of coal beside the trapdoor), and went off on the snick-an-lurk.

I was alone. I went to the parapet and looked down for Shot-in-the-Head. I saw numerous ragged, scabby heads and hulking shoulders drifting by, like rubbish in a deep ditch; but Shot-in-the-Head must have gone too close by the wall.

I shivered. It was cold, so high up in the air. I went back to the fire and coughed over it, and thought of home.

Suddenly the trapdoor moved aside and out came a woman's head. It was so unexpected, and she was cut off so sharp, that it was as if a ghastly murder had been done downstairs, and the rest of her would be heaved up any minute. She saw me.

"Where is 'e? Where's Shots?"

"Gone on the snick-an-lurk," I said.

"Bleedin' little varmint," said she. "Allus missin' when yer wants 'im. You 'is mate?"

"Yes."

"Mind this, then."

She vanished and then reappeared up to her waist. She pushed a bundle onto the flat path.

"Don't you drop 'im, mind!"

It was a baby. The mother sank out of sight and the trapdoor closed over her. I supposed that she, too, had gone on the snick-an-lurk.

I picked up the baby, which gave one or two irritated cries, and put it inside the house next to the fire. I sat down and watched it, and wondered if the woman had been Shot-in-the-Head's mother. Even if she had been, I don't suppose she knew; and I don't suppose Shot-in-the-Head knew, either.

I wondered what would happen if she didn't come back, if she was caught on the snick-an-lurk, and hanged. What would I do with the baby?

I wondered if that was what had happened to Shot-in-the-Head—that he'd been left on a roof in the charge of another Shot-in-the-Head, who'd been stuck with him thereafter.

These thoughts occupied me until Shot-in-the-Head came back with a loaf of bread and a lump of raw meat. He saw the baby and said: "You oughter 'ave fixed 'im."

He produced a long piece of cord and tied one end round the baby's middle, and the other round his own.

" 'E gits abaht," said Shot-in-the-Head with unwilling admiration. "Quick as a pidjin. You should see 'im! I thort 'e'd never move at fust. Then 'e started. All at once, it was. I nearly lorst 'im. Yus."

He gazed on the parapet, and I got a sudden picture of Shot-in-the-Head hanging on to the baby by one of its feet.

Soon after, the baby's owner came back. She produced a jug of ale.

"Brung extry fer yer mate, Shots," she said; and took her property away.

"Me mates is arter yer," said Shot-in-the-Head, passing me the jug after he'd had a drink. "Liverguts 'as got a squashed-in eye orf Mr. Rob-a-Son fer losin' yer. Squashed right in, it is. 'E'll 'ave yer wiv' that 'ook, I ken tell yer! Yus."

I shivered. Shot-in-the-Head said:

"If yer wants to keep warm wiv'out bein' spifflicated by the smoke, yer wants to sit up agin the pots. They's allus warm."

He didn't go out again that day. He cooked the meat and divided the loaf into three: one part for himself, one for me, and the last between two starlings, Pankuss and Mary Bone, who seemed to be friends of his and perched in his hair.

He showed me round his estate, which extended for about six roofs in all directions. He was very proud of it and pointed out various beauties of the landscape, such as the sudden jeweled sight of the river, winking between clustering stacks.

But most of all, he admired St. Paul's which sometimes, he said, made him laugh.

As he pointed to the great dome I began to realize that, from its situation relative to the river, I could not be far from Mr. Seed's.

"Is this," I said uneasily, "in Whitefriars?"

"Yus. You wanna watch yerself dahn there."

I grew colder than ever as I remembered Mrs. Carwardine and Mrs. Branch and their tales of Whitefriars where screams were as common as dirt, where dead men lay in the gutters as frequent as cats, and where people went in and never came out.

"Do—do they really cut you up down there?"

"Yus," said Shot-in-the-Head. "But allus very small."

That night I didn't sleep so well. Every noise I heard coming up from the street, I thought was a murder being done; every sound of dripping, I thought was blood; and every shadow that passed across the roof and loitered by the chimney-stacks, I thought was Liverguts with his hook.

Next morning was Sunday, and the air was bright with bells. They rang and chimed and pealed and rolled, and none of us could speak. Shot-in-the-Head put his hands to his ears and only took them away to shake his fists at St. Paul's. Then he opened his mouth and made a little belfry of it, and tolled his tongue inside.

In the afternoon he went on the snick-an-lurk again; and back came the baby for me to mind. This time I tied it up properly, and tried to get it to move.

Shot-in-the-Head came back with a gold-topped cane and three meat pies; and we got an apronful of coals for the baby, and a complaint about coal smuts in its eye.

That evening I sat by the fire with Shot-in-the-Head, and we talked and talked till the cows came home, wherever that might have been in the town. He only stopped me when the sun went down, and that was because he wanted to show me the western rooftops all torn up with red.

Then I went on and told him about my house, and Woodbury, and Hertford, and the trees and fields and streams.

I told him everything; about my Uncle Turner, my mother and sisters, and even Mrs. Alice. I told him about the footsteps and the watch, and about my running away.

It was all a marvelous tale to him, as he sat with the red light on his face, and hanging on to every word. And when I came at last to him, he got enormously excited, and begged me to begin again.

Most of all he loved the footsteps, and the parts about my uncle. Cissy, Rebecca and my mother he quite dismissed as belonging to those parts of a story which were necessary, but dull. He liked Mrs. Alice and the raisin wine, and had quite a soft spot for Mrs. Small and her horror of leaves.

At last he went to sleep, murmuring drowsily that he would hear it all again tomorrow night; and I felt like the person in the Arabian Nights, whose life hung by the thread of an endless tale.

He himself was like something out of the Arabian Nights, with his little cave filled with glittering treasures; and I remember thinking once that, when Christmas came, we could hang all the gold and jewels from the buttonholes, and when the snow fell, we could huddle by the fire like shepherds, awaiting the wonderful news.

I felt a little sad, I admit, when I thought about Christmas, and my mother and my sisters, all of whom must have supposed me to be dead. But then I comforted myself and thought that they'd get over it, and think a good deal better of me for being in heaven. When you are living on a rooftop, among birds and chimney pots, in a small private residence, with the sky for a garden and a baby to mind, it's hard to worry much about what's happening on the ground.

I don't know how long I might have lived up there with Shot-in-the-Head, eating and drinking and exploring the roofs. It might have been forever. The nights by the fire were best of all, when I told him about my home, and he told me of his adventures down below, during the day. In the end, it was the watch that stopped it.

He had laid out all his possessions and had invited me to add mine. I took out my watch. It was just after eleven o'clock. He wanted to wind it up. I told him it was only to be six turns; but of course he couldn't count.

He wound and wound until there came a sharp little snapping noise, as if something had broken inside. I got angry and snatched it away. He got angry and snatched it back. He looked at it and shook it and got out his knife. He opened the back.

"Yus," he said. "I sees."

He gave it back to me. There was a small piece of paper wedged inside the lid. I took it out and unfolded it. There was writing on it. "Club Cottage. Shoulder of Mutton Alley. Limehouse Hole."

I stared at it, not understanding. And then, little by little, I remembered how my father had given me the watch. I remembered how he had told me how valuable it was.

Suddenly I realized why he'd given it to me. He must have known that, sooner or later I'd find what he'd hidden inside. This was the only written thing he'd left me. These were really his last words.

I wondered briefly why he hadn't told me at once? Then I remembered all his hesitations, and I guessed he'd thought I wasn't ready yet for whatever it was that I would find . . . in Club Cottage, Shoulder of Mutton Alley, Limehouse Hole.

There was no help for it. My rooftop life was over; and the ground and all its concerns were dragging me back.

What was there in Club Cottage? Was it the lost ten thousand pounds; or something else, something he valued even more?

16

LIMEHOUSE HOLE was six fingers down the River Thames. I didn't know whether this meant six miles, six hours or six shillings by waterman's boat, as Shot-in-the-Head represented everything in terms of his fingers. If he was going out, it would be for two fingers; if he wanted to tell me where he'd got something (on the snick-an-lurk), it was four fingers to the right.

As I had no money—having thrown away my purse that night in the Sun in Splendour—I was to be taken back to Mr. Seed's house; which, it turned out, was just five fingers away.

We left the roof at I don't know what time, as my watch seemed to have died. We had waited until everything was quiet; I think it must have been long after one o'clock.

It was a clear night; the clearest I can remember in London. There was a quarter moon and you could even see some stars.

Shot-in-the-Head went down the trapdoor first, and I followed after. As I began to descend, I took one last look round what had been my home for, I suppose, seven fingers.

Shot-in-the-Head's fire glowed mysteriously inside his house; and beyond, the chimney shadows divided up the roofs into long narrow slices. As I pulled the trapdoor back into place, I fancied that St. Paul's tipped its enormous hat to me, as if to say, "Pleased to have met you."

I wanted to say the same, having got into the habit, during my days of being alone, or minding the baby, of talking to objects like St. Paul's, one or two well-dressed steeples and several affable chimney pots.

I felt Shot-in-the-Head tug sharply on my foot, so down the ladder I went, into the swaying dark. He never said a word to me. It was all kicks and pinches as it had been when first he'd taken me up into his residence.

The house sighed and moaned and grunted, as before; and the rubbish on the landings stirred.

Outside in the street, it was odd; after the roofs, it was like being in a pit. We began to walk.

I could hear nothing beyond our own breathing and soft steps;

but I thought Shot-in-the-Head was worried. He kept stopping and sniffing the air, as if he'd found one smell that was worse than all the rest.

I didn't think he was frightened, I thought he was just being cautious; so that when he suddenly gripped my arm with tremendous fierceness, I was taken by surprise and began:

"What's the—"

Instantly he put his hand over my mouth. There was a moment's silence; and then, sweet and clear, and not very far away, came the old familiar whistling:

> *"I care for nobody, no, not I;*
> *And nobody cares for me!"*

There was no time to be amazed, or to wonder at the strength of John Diamond's hatred that made him haunt the streets, still looking for me. Shot-in-the-Head pointed to the beginning of a black slit between the tenements and gave me a violent push. It was the way back to Hanging Sword Alley.

I began to run. Already I could hear the other whistles, the needle-sharp whistles of the boys. I heard the scattering of the little hailstones; and then I heard the most hideous and dreadful screech.

It was the same screech I'd heard when the dwarf had caught Shot-in-the-Head and dragged him up the stairs in his house.

The hailstorm stopped; and so did I. I looked back. Liverguts and his friends had caught Shot-in-the-Head. They must have seen him cheat them by letting me go; and, like John Diamond himself, their hatred had boiled over.

They had him against a wall. I saw the iron hook lifted up in the air; and then I heard the screech again. It went right through me.

Although it was almost certain that they'd killed him already, I had to go back. There was nothing I could do; I knew that. But it was impossible not to try.

I ran a little way back and shouted out:

"I'm here! I'm here! William Jones is here! This way!"

I paused just long enough for them to turn, and then bolted for my life back through the slit.

I could hear them beginning to run; but I had nearly a dozen yards start. Down the passage I rushed, with the hailstorm in pursuit. I crashed against the close, rough walls and dragged myself round corners; until at last, a fully grown man—a man, thank God! and not a boy—stepped out into my path. With a great cry of relief I flung myself into his arms. They folded round me.

"Pleased to meet you, William Jones," he said.

It was John Diamond!

I won't tell you how I felt; but I can promise you that I've never felt worse in my life.

I did the only thing I could. I bit his wrist. He wasn't wearing gloves and I remember he smelled and tasted of soap; which I have never liked since.

He let me go. I fell on the ground and heard the hailstorm roar. John Diamond kicked me in the head; and, in the middle of shooting, dancing stars, I remembered Mrs. Carwardine and shrieked and shrieked:

"BOARDERS! BOARDERS! BOARDERS!"

I don't suppose I can really remember it; but I still have a looming sensation of doors and windows opening and huge, lumbering shapes with murderers' faces and harsh pirates' hands come crowding in upon me as the inhabitants of Whitefriars emerged to answer the cry for Sanctuary.

17

I MUST HAVE SAID something about Mr. Seed, or else my shout of "Boarders!" had identified me as belonging to his household, because I have a confused recollection of being passed through his doorway by I don't know how many strange hands, and being received by I don't know how many more.

"Mind his head! Mind his head!"

"Oh what a sight he looks!"

"Like somethin' the cat's brought in!"

"That's enough of that, you two—or you'll feel the back of me 'and!"

I saw the two Miss Carwardines, all curl-papers and skinny arms twined in complicated patterns round each other's necks. And there was Mr. Seed, in cap and nightgown, jumping up and down and apparently in a great rage.

I tried to explain that I was sorry for having got him out of bed; but that it had been a matter of the greatest urgency and I had nearly been killed.

"What's he saying? What's he talking about?"

"Oh the poor young gentleman! I'll go and fetch some soup!"

"His head! Look at that bruise! He's been kicked . . ."

"Maybe they kicked some sense into it! Here, let me look."

The dwarf was bending over me, with a candle as bright as the sun. I was lying in his bed and I could feel his short thick fingers touching my head very gently.

"Oh! Oh! 'Is lovely clothes! That coat'll never be the same!"

"No bones broken. Solid right through, I shouldn't wonder!"

"I could sew it up for five shillin's, maybe . . ."

"He ain't got five shillings, Mrs. Branch. He ain't got five pence. He's been skinned, like a rabbit!"

Faces, faces . . . looming over me and going away. I said to them that I hadn't been robbed but had thrown away my purse in the Sun in Splendour. I said we all had to go back at once, not to the Sun in Splendour, but to pick up what was left of Shot-in-the-Head.

"Kicked, dear, kicked. You was *kicked* in the head. You wasn't shot, you know . . ."

I said I wanted to go to Club Cottage in Limehouse Hole. I wanted to go directly. There wasn't a moment to be lost.

"Be quiet there! Be quiet! I can't hear a word he's saying!"

"Put that down, you two! Or I'll smack you both till your ears fly off."

I repeated my determination to go back into Whitefriars and find Shot-in-the-Head; but somehow mixed it up with John Diamond and Limehouse Hole. In order to make it clear to everybody, I tried to whistle "The Miller of Dee," and to explain about the baby on the roof that had begun to worry me greatly.

"Deleterious," said Mrs. Branch. "That's what 'e is. Poor Mr. Branch was like it in 'is cups. Very deleterious."

"Thank God, I say, and I'll say it again! Thank God 'e left one good shirt be'ind and a pair of stockin's, too," said Mrs. Carwardine; and I couldn't help feeling that, although everybody was glad I was back, their joy was rather gloomed over by the state of my clothes. It was as if it wasn't really me who had returned, but a friend bringing my tattered remains.

Mr. Seed was sitting next to me with a satisfied smile on his face that quickly changed into sternness when he saw that I was awake. It was morning.

"That's a shilling you owe me, Mr. Jones," he said. "And seven shillings and sixpence to Mrs. Carwardine and Mrs. Branch for work on your clothes. How do you propose to pay?"

"My watch," I said. "I've still got my watch."

"Broken," said he. "Spring gone. Cost a mint to put it right."

"I'd better go then," I said; and tried to get out of bed.

He pushed me back and told me that my clothes had already gone for repairs and he wasn't going to have me running about outside on a Saturday morning stark naked. It would get him a bad name.

"But I must go!" I cried, thinking suddenly of Shot-in-the-Head, lying somewhere in Whitefriars and maybe still alive.

"Must," said Mr. Seed, "is for the king."

I told him he didn't understand, and that I had urgent business in Whitefriars concerning a certain boy who had saved my life. I begged him to fetch my clothes and let me go.

He shook his head. He told me that the men who had brought me back had scattered all the boys. I'd never find the one I wanted though I searched till Kingdom Come. If he'd been killed, he'd be in the river by now; if not, he'd be hiding like a rat.

I knew he was right, that I'd never find Shot-in-the-Head again; but I was far from satisfied. In fact, I felt miserably unhappy and, not for the first time, cursed my father's watch and all that it had brought me. If I hadn't found the paper, then most likely I'd still be up among the chimney pots with Shot-in-the-Head; and better off than now.

The paper! Club Cottage! How strange it was that I'd forgotten it! Yet not so long ago it had been the most important thing in the world! Not so long ago, I'd wanted to make my Uncle Turner eat his words; I'd wanted to find Mr. Alfred Diamond, then John Diamond, then Club Cottage and maybe ten thousand pounds. Now it was only Shot-in-the-Head. I suppose, as my schoolmaster would have said, I lacked concentration.

There came a knock at the door. It was Mrs. Branch with a bowl of timid soup. She seemed to make soup as the rain makes mud, absolutely without thinking about it. I wondered how much it would cost.

Mr. Seed nodded; and Mrs. Branch, reassured, gave me the bowl and departed. I began to spoon away.

"I don't want to pry, Mr. Jones," said the dwarf, looking very much as if he did. "I know you like to keep your secrets. But you owe me money, Mr. Jones. You're not a person of independent means. Last night you mentioned a certain John Diamond, and a certain Club Cottage and Limehouse Hole. You talked about Shot-in-the-Head and a baby on a roof. Now it's no good saying that these are private matters. That won't do. You must tell me everything, Mr. Jones . . . because you owe me money."

He scowled ferociously and made it as plain as he could that he was a relentless creditor and was determined to be paid. In other words, he was human enough to be eaten up with curiosity and wasn't going to leave me alone until I'd told him all.

So I told him, and it was a great relief. I told him everything, right from the beginning, from the time before my father died.

He sat beside me, listening carefully, with his stubby fingers spread across his stubby knees. He nodded his head.

"I thought as much," he kept saying, no matter how striking the turns my story took. "I guessed it was something like that. Of course . . . of course . . ."

Little by little, I found myself growing irritated with him, as he couldn't possibly have guessed. Nobody could. Once or twice I thought about inventing something really wild, just to catch him out; and I was particularly annoyed when I got to the part about finding the paper in the watch.

"Of course! Naturally!" he said. "I thought so all the time!"

"How?" I said. "How did you do that? *I* didn't!"

"Oh," said he deeply. "I have thoughts where those that have overgrowed only have skin and bone. I have finger thoughts, and arm thoughts, and leg thoughts." He held up each article as he mentioned it. "I can think where you can only wear your clothes!"

There was simply no surprising him. I think if I'd sprouted wings and flown out of the window, he'd have nodded and said: "I thought it might turn out like that!" I wondered if this was because, when first he'd seen himself in a mirror, he'd got such a shock that nothing ever after could really amount to much.

"So now it's come down to Club Cottage," he said. "That's to be the answer to everything. All the way down the river to Lime-house Hole. And what do you think you'll find?"

"I don't know."

"Haven't you any ideas, Mr. Jones?"

I thought; and suggested that it might be the ten thousand pounds. Even as I said it, I felt uncomfortably that it was rather a mercenary thing to have said, and that I ought to have been more spiritual somehow. But when you are twelve, and lying in a narrow bed, with no clothes, and with a fierce creditor bending over you, ten thousand pounds *is* quite spiritual.

But Mr. Seed took it in good part. After all, *he* was fond of money.

"And what would you do with it?"

I thought deeply.

"Would you restore it to John Diamond?"

I shook my head.

"Would you, say, give it to me?"

It was impossible for him not to look hopeful, and equally im-possible for me not to disappoint him. He shrugged his shoulders.

"Tomorrow," he said. "Mr. Carwardine will take us down to Limehouse Hole in his boat. Then we'll see what there is in Club Cottage, and whether it's been worth the journey."

He went away and left me a prisoner in his room. Suddenly I had the mean thought that he was off to Club Cottage to take whatever he could find. I wondered if that was why he'd tried to warn me that I might find nothing there.

Almost at once I felt ashamed of thinking it, particularly when Mrs. Carwardine told me about the terrible distraction my absence had caused.

She came in with my good shirt and hung it over the chair and stood admiring it in a melancholy sort of way, as if it was me as an angel.

She smoothed it and patted it and told me that everybody had been sure that I was killed on account of my clothes and gold watch and that I'd turn up at Deptford or Wapping Old Stairs and that Mr. Carwardine had been keeping a sharp lookout for me and had once thought he'd seen me floating past Billingsgate but that I'd turned out to be a dog.

And there was Mr. Seed running about all over the town looking for me and even asking Mr. K'Nee, who'd thought I'd gone back to my home and so had that Mr. Needleman and somebody in the Horse Boy, which was a place Mr. Seed never liked on account of them stuck-up clerks. But *he'd* known all along that I wasn't dead and when I'd been fetched in, in the middle of the night, by them cutthroats from Whitefriars with my head kicked in, he hadn't been in the least surprised.

"Now don't touch nothin', you two!" she said, as the two Miss Carwardines drifted in together, unwound themselves, and drifted about separately.

They were called—and I don't know why—Butter and Cress, Butter being the taller; and you certainly had to keep your eye on them. They couldn't leave anything alone, and they fought like cats when one got hold of something first.

Butter got hold of my watch; and Cress pulled her hair. I said I'd call Mr. Seed if they didn't put it down.

"Dirty little telltale!" said Butter; and at once the Miss Carwardines were friends.

"Don't 'e look a fright," said Cress.

"Serve 'im right," said Butter.

Cress got hold of my shirt. Butter kicked her. I told them again that I'd shout for Mr. Seed. If ever two girls were born to go on the snick-an-lurk, they were the two Miss Carwardines; and it was misery lying there, with the blanket pulled up to my neck and wondering when they would try to nick that; I mean, the blanket.

It was only Mrs. Baynim who put them off. She came in to see me and the two Miss Carwardines went out of the room sideways, like carvings on the wall. I suppose they were really quite separate, but I always saw them together, united in friendship or war.

It was a great honor to be visited by Mrs. Baynim, who generally kept herself to herself, like a very refined friend. She stood in the doorway and stared at me; and I tried to look honored and pitiful at the same time.

"Hm! So much for your fine feathers, Mr. Jones," she said, after asking me how I did, and not waiting for a reply. "Better to have been a beggar to start with, than a proud person come down."

I never saw Mr. Baynim. I could only suppose that I was beneath his notice altogether.

I didn't sleep at all that night; my mind was too full of Club Cottage. It was stuffed so full of bank notes that it looked like a thatched cushion; it was full of jewels; my father was in it. He hadn't died at all, and there he was, waiting at the door! Or Shot-in-the-Head, with a mug of ale. Then my thoughts took a gloomier turn. Club Cottage had vanished; it had fallen down Limehouse Hole. Or worse, Liverguts was there with his hook; and John Diamond was standing behind the door!

"Any ideas?" said Mr. Seed, when he came in to wake me in the morning. "Any ideas about what we might find?"

"None, Mr. Seed. None at all."

At ten o'clock, we went to church and after that we were to go down to Mr. Carwardine's boat. My clothes looked quite presentable; but I must admit I cut a poor figure beside all the Carwardines, and Mrs. Baynim and Mrs. Branch, who were all highly decorated. I felt rather sad that I could no longer be a credit to them, and had to be hidden in the middle.

The service seemed to go on forever; and the only items of interest were that the two Miss Carwardines got hit for poking their fingers into the poor box, and Mrs. Branch was sure that she'd seen Mr. Branch on the other side of the aisle. Unfortunately he'd vanished before she could get to him; but she thought he'd looked thinner than before.

When we got back, Mr. Seed had some food ready; but I couldn't eat it, so he put it in a basket for our journey down the river.

We were gathered at the foot of the stairs and there was a great fuss going on as Butter and Cress wanted to come on the boat and kept screaming that Mr. Carwardine was their pa and it was his boat and therefore they had a better right than me.

Mrs. Carwardine was threatening them with the back of her hand and Mr. Carwardine was threatening them with the front of his, bunched up in a fist.

"I won't 'ave it!" shouted Mrs. Carwardine. "I won't be shamed! I'll—"

"What's that!"

"What?"

"That there!"

"Don't touch it! It's somethin' to do with them 'orrible boys!"

A folded piece of paper had suddenly come under the front door. Immediately Mrs. Carwardine rushed to the back of the hall and began thumping on the wall with her broomstick.

"Pig! Villain!" she shouted. "And on a Sunday, too!"

Back came the angry voice: "I'll have the law on you! So help me, I will!"

Mr. Seed picked up the paper. It was a letter, neatly sealed. He gave it to me. It was addressed to William Jones Esquire. A little frightened, I broke the seal and opened it. The writing was small and rather cramped.

"Dear Mr. Jones," it began.

It having come to the writer's attention that you are now residing at a certain premises in Hanging Sword Alley, off Fleet Street, and are in good health, the writer firstly requires your absolute discretion in the matter of his identity, which must remain forever INCOGNITO.

Secondly, the writer wishes to inform you that a certain person, again INCOGNITO, does not wish to be associated, in word or deed with another person in that other person's felonious intentions towards your goodself.

Thirdly, the writer wishes to make it plain that the above-mentioned innocent party renounces here and now and entirely any connection with the other party of the said felonious intent. He, the innocent party, deeply regrets any inconvenience that might have been caused to your goodself and hopes that, if the matter should come to court, you will see your way clear to giving evidence on his behalf.

Fourthly, the writer wishes to inform you that inquiries have

been made after your goodself in a certain place by a person
from Hertford. As these Inquiries were made on Friday
last, which was before the writer was aware of your present
place of residence, he was unable to furnish a satisfactory
answer to the person from Hertford and therefore had no choice,
pending Corpus Delicti, but to presume the decease of your
goodself.

Fifthly, the writer wishes to inform you that the above
information was obtained from the aforesaid innocent party by
means of threatening behavior on the part of the person of felonious
intent. In consequence of this, the felonious person has this day
departed for Hertford.

I remain, dear sir, your well-wisher and friend, INCOGNITO.

I read it twice over and was beginning again, when Mr. Seed took it out of my hand. He read it once, and scowled.

"What does it mean?" I asked. "Who is it from?"

"I don't think there's much doubt," said he, "that it's from our friend Mr. Jenkins. And it means that he's been smitten with conscience and cold feet. He's frightened to death of what John Diamond was going to do, and he wants to be well out of the way. That's what it means, Mr. Jones. And I suppose we should honor him for having some spark of human feeling. That's the fatty part of the letter. The meaty part is that John Diamond has taken himself off to Hertford."

At once I felt the most enormous sense of relief! This was the best news ever. Knowing nothing of Club Cottage, he'd gone to Hertford in search of me. The nightmare of finding him waiting had been removed!

I thought no more about John Diamond, or what there might be in his dark and desperate mind. I thought only of Club Cottage and what I would find.

18

LIMEHOUSE HOLE lay on a broad bend in the river, four miles down from Whitefriars Stairs. It lay past London Bridge, past the Tower, past Wapping and Execution Dock, and down among a welter of shipping and a winter of masts.

It was all narrow docks and little wooden bridges, and row upon row of neat young cottages that looked, somehow, as if they meant to grow up into better houses than the gaunt old tenements of the town.

I couldn't see a Hole anywhere; but suddenly one seemed to open up inside me when Mr. Seed gripped my arm and said:

"Here it is, Mr. Jones. This is the street."

It stretched alongside a quiet dock in which a ship seemed to have fallen asleep on its side. It was a bright little street of no more than a dozen whitewashed houses; and *they* seemed to have fallen asleep in the afternoon sun.

I never saw such a peaceful, retired-looking street; I never saw a street less likely to be hiding ten thousand pounds. I'd expected something dark and secret; I'd expected to be uneasy and frightened; I think I'd expected ghosts.

I felt bitterly, miserably disappointed; and all the hopes I'd built up vanished down Jones's Hole, which was a good deal deeper than any that might have been in Limehouse.

Club Cottage was the house on the corner. It had two bay windows and looked as if nothing was further from its mind than having been inside my father's watch.

I think I might have gone away without doing anything, if Mr. Seed hadn't been so inquisitive himself and pushed me forward to knock on the door.

A woman in a cap and apron came to answer it.

"Well?" said she, looking at me and Mr. Seed in some surprise. "What do you want?"

I tried to look past her, to see if there was money coming out of the walls; but everything looked so clean and neat that I doubted if the morning's dust was still there, let alone a secret that was twenty years old.

"I can't stand here all day," she said. "What do you want?"

I don't know why, but I found her question impossible to answer. I suppose I'd expected Club Cottage to know *me*; and not the other way round.

The woman kept staring at Mr. Seed.

"I'm a dwarf, ma'am!" he snapped angrily. "This is all I've growed. Name of Seed. Fell on stony ground, you know. He's a boy. End up taller than you, most likely. Name of Jones. Mr. Seed and Mr. Jones, ma'am."

She grew red in the face and went away. We waited. I heard her say something about, "Dwarf an' a boy, sir," and then a voice murmuring in reply. She came back.

"The master says for you to come in."

We were shown into the parlor. There were two elderly gentlemen sitting at a table in front of the fire. They were playing at cards.

To my amazement, one of them was Mr. K'Nee! The other was white-haired and long-faced, as if he'd been losing. For a moment I thought he looked faintly familiar; but it was the familiarity of resemblance, not of memory. He reminded me of somebody, but I couldn't think who. I thought he looked at me in the same way.

Mr. K'Nee stood up. He seemed to be irritated by having been discovered at his Sunday afternoon game of cards with his friend. A great many thoughts flashed through my mind to the effect that Mr. K'Nee had found the ten thousand pounds and was sitting on it; literally, I mean, that it was stuffed under the cushion of his chair.

"What brings you to Limehouse, Mr. Seed?"

Mr. Seed was irritated, too. I felt that he was angry with me for having got him into the embarrassment of being confronted by his employer.

"Go on, Mr. Jones!" he muttered. "Give him that paper out of the watch!"

I gave it to Mr. K'Nee. He glanced at it and handed it to his friend. The other gentleman shrugged his shoulders and murmured something about "a voice from the grave."

Mr. K'Nee folded the paper carefully and gave it back to me.

"I see the prodigal returned," he said, looking at me but still speaking to Mr. Seed, as if the dwarf was my keeper and I'd just been brought up from the cells.

"Half dead," said Mr. Seed. "On Friday night. Half dead, sir."

"Which half? The top, I imagine."

I don't think he was referring to the bruise on my head, but to the fact that he thought I was a fool.

The white-haired gentleman consulted the cards he was holding. I don't think they could have been good ones as he looked rather mournful.

"And where did you go, David Jones's son?" asked Mr. K'Nee, speaking to me for the first time. "Where have you been all these days?"

What an ugly old man he was! And what a clever one. Although, by rights, I was the one who ought to have been asking the questions, he had turned it round completely. I felt like a criminal.

"I—I—"

"Yes. We know that. You. You. Come along. Answer the question."

The white-haired gentleman made an odd noise. It was a chuckle. I hated both of them. I thought they were a pair of old demons, enjoying the destruction of my hopes.

Then Mr. Seed came to my rescue. I suppose he felt he had to justify himself as well as me. He was, I always noticed, a very proud little man and disliked being put on a level with a boy.

"Mr. Jones here," said Mr. Seed, "was nearly murdered." And he went on to tell the story I'd told him. He told about the way I'd been tricked and hunted down and my hiding on the roof in Whitefriars. He told about Shot-in-the-Head and the deep hatred of John Diamond.

I interrupted where I could, as I felt that the dwarf was not making a good impression. Mr. K'Nee was looking angrier and angrier and he kept glancing at his friend, who was fiddling with the cards in his hand and looking more mournful than ever.

All this time we had been left standing. The servant had come in once, but Mr. K'Nee had waved her away. I remember someone passed by the window in front of the house. He must have glanced in, because the white-haired gentleman smiled in a pained sort of way.

"So you've had a bad time of it," said Mr. K'Nee, when Mr. Seed finished. "Well, bad times are best for the young. You would have been better off to have stayed at home and been a good son to your mother."

"I couldn't stay   "

"—Couldn't? Come, come, David Jones's son! Was it so hard to be a good son?"

The white-haired gentleman put down his cards. I noticed that his knuckles were bony with pressing down.

"He couldn't!" said Mr. Seed firmly. "And that's the long and short of it, if you'll pardon the expression, Mr. K'Nee!"

"How's that, Mr. Seed?"

The dwarf told him. He told him everything he knew about me. I think he told it rather well, even though he was inclined to give me the credit for better feelings than I knew I had.

But I put up with it; and learned, with some surprise, that my chief hope all the time had been to right a past wrong and that all I'd ever wanted was to restore to John Diamond everything his father had lost. Generously he played down my interest in the ten thousand pounds and my fear and dislike of my Uncle Turner (which, I suppose, had really driven me out of my house), and represented me as quite a shining boy, such as I myself would have jeered at and poured ink in his hair at school.

Anyway, as I listened to Mr. Seed, I found my story to be truly remarkable; and I couldn't help waiting anxiously for what would happen next.

Mr. K'Nee and his friend, however, did not seem so amazed. They nodded in exactly the same way as Mr. Seed had done when I'd told him; and murmured:

"Of course . . . of course!" in exactly the same tone of voice.

I began to feel that there was a general conspiracy of the old never to be surprised by the young; only to be angry and distressed. Certainly the white-haired gentleman looked to be both.

He fidgeted in his chair, scowled at Mr. K'Nee and Mr. Seed, and then fixed his eyes on somewhere between my neck and the bottom of my waistcoat.

"So," he muttered; and it was the first time he spoke to me. "You came across this—this Mr. Robinson."

"Diamond!" I said. "He was John Diamond all the time!"

"Robinson. I prefer to call him Robinson."

"But his name is Diamond, sir!"

"Not so far as I am concerned," said the white-haired gentleman quietly. He picked up his cards and studied them again. Then he said, to the cards, it seemed: "It looks like David Jones was lucky to the last, K'Nee. He had the Ace; and I had the Knave."

He looked straight into my face.

"I am that—that young scoundrel's father," he said. "I am Alfred Diamond!"

19

"WELL?" SAID MR. K'NEE, after an enormous pause in which various things sank into my mind and made a dull commotion there, like Algebra.

For instance: the heart of the mystery had turned out to be nothing more than a bubble of peace and quiet in which two old gentlemen were playing at cards, and I was interrupting them; Mr. Seed was gazing out of the window and trying to look as if he had nothing to do with me; and Mr. K'Nee had just put his hands behind his back and thrust out his clenched-up fist of a face towards me as if he was going to punch me with it.

"Well?" he repeated. "Now you know it. The person you came to Foxes Court to find, is sitting in front of you. That is Mr. Alfred Diamond. I will give you an Affidavit to that effect."

I felt that something extraordinary was expected of me, something to the effect that I had discovered the secret of life and was about to reveal it; otherwise, what was I doing there, standing in the middle of the carpet like an ornamental boy made out of wood?

"What do you want with him?" demanded Mr. K'Nee, advancing his face another inch. "You may tell me. I am his lawyer. I conduct all his business. Do you want him to go to your home and justify you before your uncle? Is that what you want?"

I examined the wall across which the dying sun had cast a pattern of the window. I got no help from it.

"Or was it just to say that your poor father died regretting what he'd done? Well—we know that. David Jones was human, like the rest of us. May he rest in peace."

Mr. K'Nee's face came forward yet another inch, and so suddenly that I started back.

"Or did you have some idea of that ten thousand pounds?"

I had; but didn't say so.

"Well," said Mr. K'Nee harshly, "there is no ten thousand pounds. There never was. It was a clerk's dream; nothing more. Ah! You look downcast! Boys and fools will always dream of hidden treasure. That's their nature. Grown men have better sense."

I began to feel very depressed. While the dwarf had told my story, I'd thought I'd made a good impression and my virtues had shone as bright as waistcoat buttons; but now the lawyer seemed to get right to the heart of the matter and I didn't feel virtuous at all. Nevertheless, I did feel some stirrings of anger.

"But—but it was you who told me about it . . ."

"Ah! So that's it! Well, well! I told you that Mr. Diamond was dead, too! Remember that?"

"But why—?"

"Bring me a Subpoena! Bring me an Order of Court! Then I'll tell you why! Until then, be satisfied that you're still alive. You've done quite enough for a boy of twelve. You've caused quite enough distress and injury. I don't speak of what you've done in your own home; I speak of here and now. You have put Mr. Seed to a great deal of inconvenience and expense—"

"Eleven shillings and sixpence to date, Mr. K'Nee," chimed in the dwarf, as quickly as a shop-door bell.

"Eleven shillings and sixpence," repeated Mr. K'Nee. "And—and you have caused my client considerable unhappiness by reminding him of someone he would rather forget. I speak of Mr. Robinson."

"That's enough, K'Nee; that's enough," said Mr. Diamond. "The boy is very distressed. He doesn't understand . . ."

"What is there to understand?" demanded Mr. K'Nee fiercely.

"The money—"

"What money?"

Suddenly Mr. K'Nee looked furtive and almost guilty. My hopes rose.

"The money, K'Nee. He'll find out anyway. You'd better tell him."

So there was money after all! My heart thundered. I couldn't help it. It was, as the lawyer had said, in the nature of boys and fools to dream of hidden treasure; and, by the brightening up of Mr. Seed's face, it was in the nature of dwarfs, too.

But where was it? Helplessly I looked round the room and caught Mr. Seed's brightly hopeful eye. Poor dwarf! Little did he know what was coming.

"Very well," said Mr. K'Nee. "There is some money. As they say, there's no smoke without fire. But before you make plans for spending it, remember that smoke often exaggerates the flame. The ten thousand pounds, David Jones's son, is a good deal nearer two thousand. Say two thousand pounds, give or take a hundred, put out at compound interest of the imagination for twenty years, and there you have your ten thousand. Leave it another twenty years and it will be a million! So how will you have it, David Jones's son? In bank notes, or in dreams? Take it in bank notes and it will be no more than a thousand pounds; for half of it belongs to Mr. Diamond here. Take it in dreams, and you can keep it all."

He drew breath, and I felt that I was standing on my heart—so far had it dropped!

Mr. K'Nee went on; and he told me where and what the money really was. It was the house in Hanging Sword Alley, at the back of Twiss's Coffee. It was the house where Mr. Seed lived. It was where my father and Mr. Diamond had first set up in business; and it still belonged to Mr. Diamond and my father's estate.

By some oversight of Deeds, it had not been included in the sale of the business to Mr. Twiss. Although the premises, as bricks and mortar, weren't worth much, it was worth a great deal to Mr. Twiss; and it was he who'd offered the two thousand pounds, give or take a hundred.

So there was the glittering dream of Mr. Jenkins and Mr. Needleman and maybe a dozen other dreamers round about Foxes Court. A little, little treasure, so buried under Leases and Copyholds and Covenants and Agreements that a hundred lawyers working night and day for a hundred years might not have got it out intact.

I think Mr. K'Nee had kept quiet about it because he'd feared that if my father had got wind of it he'd have come back and cheated Mr. Diamond all over again. As it was, the house provided his old friend with a little income in the shape of rent from Mr. Seed as the tenant landlord.

As Mr. K'Nee said this, I looked uncomfortably at Mr. Seed;

and Mr. Seed looked uncomfortably at me. I knew he was thinking that I was his part landlord; and he was inwardly waving goodbye to his eleven shillings and sixpence.

"Well?" said Mr. K'Nee. "Will you have it in dreams, or in cash?"

"In dreams," I said; not because I wanted to, but because I didn't seem to have any choice.

Mr. K'Nee shrugged his shoulders and went over to the window. Mr. Diamond reached forward and touched my arm, as if to wake me up.

"I was sorry," he said, "to hear of your father's death. He was a good friend of mine."

"But—" I began.

"Oh yes! He cheated me. I forgot. It was such a long time ago. Now I just remember that he was my friend and that you are his son. And I'm glad to meet you, William Jones."

We shook hands. I was relieved as the thought had crossed my mind that he might hate me worse than his son had done. But it seemed that hatred was only alive in the second generation.

Mr. Diamond, guessing what I was thinking, blamed himself for his son's violence, in spite of interruptions from Mr. K'Nee who kept snapping out that John Diamond was a bad lot and that Mr. Diamond had been the best of fathers and should stop reproaching himself.

"No, no, K'Nee! If I hadn't told John about David Jones, if I hadn't planted that seed in his mind, he might have grown up quite differently. I blame myself . . . myself!"

"Blame David Jones, rather!"

Again my father! Again the footsteps and the sighs. His guilt was deeper than I'd supposed; deeper, perhaps, than he himself had known. No wonder his ghost still walked!

The blackest of gloom came over me as I realized this new—or new to me—consequence of what my father had done; and I wondered why it was that wrong seemed to breed wrong so much more easily than right bred right, as if there was something in our constitution that made such good soil for plants of the more poisonous variety.

I wondered if my father had known all along about John Diamond and that was why he'd left it to me to put matters right . . . as if he felt that it would be easier for one son to approach another. If so, I hoped that his ghost had seen what had happened on London Bridge.

Mr. Diamond rang for his housekeeper and asked her to bring in some cake. He smiled knowingly at Mr. Seed and Mr. K'Nee and said that he felt sure that cake would cheer me up. He was one of those kindly old gentlemen who think that they know all about boys and that a boy's heart desires nothing more than cake and that, in all probability, the affair of Cain and Abel would have turned out better if only Cain had been given more cake.

At about five o'clock, when it was getting quite dark, Mr. K'Nee's carriage called to take him back to London. He offered to drive me and Mr. Seed back to Hanging Sword Alley as it was too late for me to think of going back to Hertford that night.

I said I hadn't been thinking of it. Mr. K'Nee said it was high time that I had. Did I know that inquiries had been made after me in Foxes Court? I told him that I did know.

"How?"

"I had a letter, Mr. K'Nee."

"What letter?"

I showed it to him. He read it through and called Mr. Jenkins, whose hand and style he recognized, a stupid little scoundrel and a damned idiot. He began to make plans for having Mr. Jenkins committed to Newgate for the rest of his natural life when suddenly his hand shook and he bunched up his face so fiercely that his nose almost met his chin.

"What is it, K'Nee?" asked Mr. Diamond curiously.

"Nothing . . . nothing."

"What is it, K'Nee?"

"He's gone there. Your—your Mr. Robinson. He's found out where the boy lives. He's gone there, Diamond!"

At once Mr. Diamond uttered a frightful cry and hid his face in his hands! Mr. K'Nee turned on me in absolute fury.

"You fool! You stupid little fool! Now do you see what you've done by coming to London? Now do you see what you've awakened! Do you suppose that it was only *you* that—that Mr. Robinson wanted to destroy? Do you suppose a lifetime's hatred was to be satisfied with the death of a boy? When did you get this letter?"

"This—this morning, sir."

"This morning? Then maybe there's still time. Maybe. You'd better stay here, Diamond. The boy and I will go—"

"No—no! I must come! He is my son, K'Nee!"

Even then I didn't fully understand what was happening, and my chief fear was for the wrath of Mr. K'Nee. I remember as we left Club Cottage and got into Mr. K'Nee's carriage I felt thankful that Mr. Diamond was coming after all as I thought that his presence would help to shield me from the enraged lawyer.

He put his arm round my shoulder and urged me not to blame

myself. He said it was he who was to blame because he had hidden himself away.

"Don't say that, Diamond!" cried Mr. K'Nee. "I forbid you to say that! Would you take upon yourself the guilt for the murder of a whole household?"

It was only then, when Mr. K'Nee said that, that I realized the full extent of what I'd unleashed! Mr. Diamond's guilt and even my father's were as nothing compared with mine!

20

WE GOT TO HERTFORD at about ten o'clock. If only the journey had been as quick as it is to say it!

If only we hadn't had to wait so long at Waltham Cross to rest Mr. K'Nee's horses! If only it hadn't been a pitch-black night so that we had to keep stopping as Mr. K'Nee was sure the coachman had got lost! If only the coach-lamps hadn't blown out at Wormley and taken an age to light again! If only we hadn't taken a wrong turn at Ware! If only—if only—

Every second of the way I was haunted and terrified by what John Diamond might be doing in Woodbury. Already I saw all my family lying dead and most horribly slaughtered—most likely by Liverguts's hook—and only my Uncle Turner left alive.

I never thought of him dying, partly because he was only related to my father by marriage and so had nothing to do with his guilt, and partly because I felt that nothing good could ever happen to me again.

Mr. Diamond and Mr. K'Nee had come away in such a hurry that they were still holding their cards. There was an old watchman's lantern inside the coach and Mr. K'Nee was all for finishing their game. This was because he wanted to take Mr. Diamond's mind off what might be happening in Woodbury. So far as *my* mind was concerned, I think he was of the opinion that it could go to the devil. He was only concerned about Mr. Diamond, who was his client and his friend.

It turned out that he'd always done everything in his power to protect Mr. Diamond from the consequences of his dangerous son. It was he who'd made John Diamond change his name to Robinson and, I believe, had threatened him with legal proceedings if he dragged his father's name any further into the filth.

I picked all this up in scraps of conversation with Mr. Diamond as we rattled along through the dark.

"Pay attention, Diamond!" Mr. K'Nee kept snapping. "I played a trump!"

Cards were Mr. Diamond's passion; and I think it was something to do with gambling that had allowed my father to take advantage and cheat him out of the business. I don't know for sure; but I think so.

"Ah!" said Mr. Diamond, losing a trick. "There he is! There he is!"

Mr. K'Nee had just played the Knave of Diamonds, and the old gentleman stared down forlornly at the smiling face on the card. It didn't look much like the Jack of Diamonds I knew; but I, too, thought of him, and of blood running out of the windows of my home.

Poor Mr. Seed had a terrible journey. He was so short that he was bounced about like a rag doll, and never stopped inquiring dismally if we were there yet.

After Hertford I had to direct the coachman through the winding maze of country lanes. I hardly recognized them, as they looked so strange and sudden in the burrowing coach-light. Turnings appeared that I'd forgotten; and deep, obscure tunnels opened up through ghastly trees.

I was on the box, straining my eyes for the crossroads I knew so well, when Mr. K'Nee said suddenly, "Are we still in England?" He was poking his head out of the window as far as it would go. "Or is this the other side of the world?"

"Why? What do you mean?"

"There's another sunset," he said. "Over there. Through the trees."

"That's not a sunset, Mr. K'Nee," said Mr. Seed. "That's a fire."

Had the coach wheels not been making such an uproar, we would have heard it, crackling and roaring. Had the wind been blowing in another direction, we would have smelled it, suffocating the air. Had all the things that had happened to us on the way not happened, and we'd been half an hour sooner, we might have stopped it. As it was, we were too late, too late. My home was burning down to the ground!

I remember, as I saw that redness glimmering through the trees, where there should have been only darkness, a thousand horrible fears rushed through my mind, together with a huge hatred for John Diamond who had done it.

I remember, as I jumped from the carriage and crashed among

roadside bushes, and began to run and run towards Mr. K'Nee's sunset, that all I wanted was to kill John Diamond, and to tear him to pieces. In my heart of hearts I was certain that those I loved best were burned and dead.

"They're dead! They're dead! They're dead!"

Lights in the church, lights in the inn, lights in the cottages . . . but they were nothing to the dreadful light that streamed and roared from my home!

The gate was wide open and a host of black figures, lit at the edges, crowded the grass and the gravel path. All Woodbury was there! All Woodbury, in its curl-papers, shirtsleeves, blankets and nightcaps, jostling each other and pointing and gaping at my flaming house!

Where was he? Was he among the crowd? Was he leaning against the great tree in the middle of the lawn?

"Stop shoving, boy! Take your turn!"

"Let me through! Let me through!"

"Get out of the way!"

Suddenly all Woodbury's children set up a shriek of excitement as a piece of my roof came flaming down, like a bad angel, and smashed into a million sparks in front of my door. In the increase of light, I thought I saw him, grinning and pointing!

Then the wind changed and a gust of smoke rushed outwards from all the windows, as if the house had given up the ghost, and there was a gasping and a coughing and a general falling back and all Woodbury's eyes streamed with crocodile tears.

"WILLIAM!"

Somebody shouted my name! The smoke shifted. Figures stumbled.

"WILLIAM!"

It was Rebecca! It was my sister Rebecca! Had anybody told me, a month before, that I would have wept for joy at the sight of Rebecca, I would have been outraged. But I wept.

She had a coat over her nightgown and her arms were full of books. She was alive! In an instant I divined she was the only one who'd been saved! In an instant I foresaw that it would just be Rebecca and me. I would look after her forever. She would never marry; she was much too plain for that. She would keep house . . .

"WILLIAM!"

Cissy! A walking mountain of hats and gowns. Soot all over her face and her feet were bare. But alive! Rebecca sank into insignificance. I'd always preferred Cissy . . .

"WILLIAM!"

My mother! They were all alive! They rushed upon me; and I rushed upon them. And there was Mrs. Alice, carrying saucepans like iron babies. She dropped them and clutched me and my head went into her apron and rebounded like a football!

Even my Uncle Turner was safe. He was at the back of the house, commanding a bucket chain from the fishpond. The Hertford engine had been sent for, but there wasn't much hope. Everything had happened so quickly that everybody was lucky to get out alive. If Mrs. Alice hadn't imagined she'd heard somebody whistling and gone downstairs . . .

"What's the matter, William? We're all alive, dear. What is it?"

I was looking for him, for John Diamond. I knew he was there. He was in the crowd! He was watching us! But where?

"Look out! Look out there!"

All Woodbury's children shrieked again. The shutters over the window of my father's room had blazed and fallen away like bright curtains. At the same time, the glass exploded with a bang; and all Woodbury shrieked louder than ever.

Somebody was inside the room! A face as grayish white as ash—really like ash!—had stared out! Then it vanished as if it had been blown away.

"Did you see that?"

"Yes—yes! What—who was it?"

"I don't know—"

It was John Diamond! The madman was still in the house! I stared at the window. Veils of flame were coming up from the fallen shutters. Veils of flame must have been coming up from him, too.

I'd wanted him to die; and now he was about to. He was burning up in his own hatred. I tried to be pleased; but it wasn't possible. There'd been such a frightful look on his face, such a wild, wild despair that he hadn't looked like John Diamond at all. He'd looked more like my dead friend, Shot in the Head. I'd thought of that instantaneously; and then he'd gone.

He hadn't seen me. He'd been staring in quite a different direction. He'd seen something that had had a great effect on him; and it had been that *something* that had driven him back from the window and into the fire. It had been something that had frightened him more than the prospect of death.

It had been his father! Old Mr. Diamond was running and stumbling and shrieking:

"John! John! John!" and Mr. K'Nee and Mr. Seed were running after and trying to hold him back.

The dwarf had got hold of his coattails and Mr. K'Nee was

shouting: "Leave him! Leave him!" meaning John Diamond, who was beyond helping, and there was a fearful commotion going on all round them.

"My son! It's my son!" screamed the old gentleman, struggling to fight everybody off.

But even if he'd managed to get free, he wouldn't have been able to do anything. He wouldn't have got past the bucket chain that was slopping hopeless water along the front of the house. They'd have stopped him easily. There were about a dozen of them—huge people—and they'd have caught him up like a baby. And anyway, he'd never have been able to climb through the window . . .

It was hard enough even for me, and I cut my hands badly on the broken glass.

I forgot to tell you, by the way, that while everybody had turned to stare at the shouting old gentleman, I'd gone off, like a dog after a cat, straight at the house.

It had struck me, very uncomfortably, that John Diamond wasn't perishing in his own hatred but in mine; and that, even if nobody else knew it, Mr. Diamond would have known it, and after all that had happened, that would have been the worst thing in the world.

Somebody threw a bucket of water at me—not the whole bucket but just the water—in mistake for the fire, and then I was inside the room and people outside were shouting that I was mad and would be killed and I couldn't help agreeing with them.

It was absolutely frightful inside that room. Everything was smoldering: my father's bed, the floorboards and the very walls! And the noise! It sounded as if the whole house had flown into a violent temper with itself, and no longer wanted to be a house and be lived in, and was trying to stamp itself flat!

Crash—crash—crash! Down came ceilings and the old winding passages! Crash—crash—crash! Down came blazing doors, melted off their hinges! Crash—crash—crash! Footsteps with a vengeance—enormous, world-sized footsteps!

I remember thinking, in a mad haste, that this was where it had all begun—in this very room—and this was where it was all going to end.

John Diamond was still there. He was standing, pressed up against the wall by the door and smoke was pouring up all round him. He was so still and stiff that I thought he was already dead, and was just propped up, like a broom.

I shouted for him to come over to the window. He wouldn't move. He just glared at me through the smoke; and then he began coughing violently. There were people at the window behind me, throwing water to try and put the blazing shutters out.

I ran and got hold of John Diamond's sleeve. It felt harsh and charred and I burned myself on one of his buttons. I dragged at him. He came quite easily and I saw that the smoke that had been clinging to him detached itself and seemed to form another figure, pressed up against the wall. It was a gaunt, wasted figure in a suit that hung as loosely as grave-clothes

I think, by that time, somebody else had got inside, because I can remember John Diamond being hoisted through the window like a bundle of dirty washing; then it was my turn and the world outside looked weird and wonderful in our house-light, and all the trees leaped out of the night as if caught unawares by such an unnatural day.

There was a tremendous cheer. I thought it was for me, but it was for the Hertford engine that had just arrived. It was being dragged up to the front of the house and all Woodbury's children were in pursuit.

I remember feeling a pang of annoyance that the Hertford engine should have stolen my cheer, and wished that it might have waited.

John Diamond had been laid on the grass and his father and Mr. K'Nee were kneeling beside him; but before I could reach him, my mother and sisters, overflowing with worry, fondness and hats, clasped me to their various bosoms with the news that I was scorched and soaked, that my eyebrows were singed and that I was BLEEDING.

It was only from my hands, but I must have wiped them across my forehead and left great streaks of blood.

Then my mother let me go, and I went to see John Diamond, in whom I felt I had a proprietary interest as I'd saved his life. He was in no state to thank me, even if he'd wanted to; but his father did, and it seemed to me that Mr. Diamond's thanks were worth more than the lost ten thousand pounds.

Even Mr. K'Nee forsook enough of his sternness to declare that I'd done very well and that David Jones would have been proud of me. He went so far as to tell my mother and sisters so; and my mother nodded vigorously, even though she didn't know Mr. K'Nee or Mr. Diamond from Adam. It wasn't until later that everybody was introduced and the wild tale of my London adventures was properly related.

One thing, however, stays firmly in my mind. It was Mr. Seed. He kept pointing at old Mr. Diamond kneeling next to his son.

Then, unable to contain his satisfaction, he hobbled about and turned discreet cartwheels under the impression that nobody was noticing. Each time he performed one, he looked around fiercely and importantly; and then did it again.

"Good for the circulation," he explained, when he saw me watching. Then, pointing once more to the reconciled father and son, he said mysteriously:

"I rather fancy, young Mr. Jones, that you won't be hearing any of them sighs and footsteps anymore."

21

IT MUST HAVE BEEN nearly three o'clock in the morning before the fire was quite put out   and then only with the help of a change in the wind and a downpour of freezing rain.

You never saw such a melancholy sight as my two soaked sisters, wandering among the charred ruins looking for lost possessions, like a pair of girl phantoms at a tragic wedding.

The old part of the house and the part with my father's room and mine, together with the kitchen and stables, were completely gutted; but the rest was still standing.

Of course it wasn't safe to go inside as there was always a danger of the fire breaking out again. Smoke was still coming up from the embers and, from time to time, when the wind blew, a thousand bright red worms winked and wriggled among the fallen beams.

The Hertford engine, which was a red-painted box on wheels with a short leather snout, as if there was a dead elephant inside, stood pointing at the defeated fire with a general air of daring it to show so much as another flicker.

I went up to have a look at it and was joined by a boy from Woodbury I went to school with. I waited for him to ask me where I'd been and was ready with a full version of my amazing experiences to flatten him. He never asked. Instead he insisted on telling me about everything I'd missed at school and that it was a great pity that I'd been away when they'd broken up for Christmas as somebody had written something rude on the blackboard and they'd all been kept in and had smashed up a desk and a couple of windows.

I gazed at him in melancholy amazement as he rattled on about the usual fights and beatings and of how somebody had made fulminating powder in a spoon and it had gone off with a report like a cannon and frightened our master's wife out of her wits.

It never occurred to him that my news was a good deal more interesting than his. I felt weary and remote and wondered how I could ever tolerate going back to school again. I felt, as Mr. Seed would have said, four times as old as my friend, and forty times as clever. And I was sad.

So much, then, for my homecoming. I didn't even have the satisfaction of receiving my Uncle Turner's abject apology for having misjudged me. In fact, I didn't see that detestable man anywhere when I was being heroic. He'd kept well out of the way as if he knew that the spectacle of my nobility would have choked him with mortification.

The first I really saw of him was in the parlor of our village inn where we sat out the rest of that terrible night, talking and dozing in front of a kinder fire than the one that had raged outside.

I sat for a while between my two sisters; but they were hard and bony and kept fidgeting, so I transferred myself to Mrs. Alice and rested my head on the bosom of the deep, which was where her apron swelled like a wave.

"Ah! He's asleep," said she, peering down at me with her round, wrinkled face that seemed, like her bosom, to have gone into the floating business. "He's fast asleep!"

I denied it and continued to take an intelligent interest in the conversation, which was about how John Diamond had got inside our house. Mrs. Alice thought it must have been through the kitchen door, which she always left open in case I came back in the middle of the night.

Here I saw my Uncle Turner's face light up with grim satisfaction, as if he'd known all along that the calamity had been something to do with me.

"I could have climbed through a window," I said, meaning to exonerate myself.

"Ssh! Ssh! Little pitchers!"

Nobody knew why John Diamond had been in my father's room, but it was supposed he'd hidden there when he'd heard Mrs. Alice. She remembered shutting all the doors to prevent the fire spreading, and she might have bolted them, too, but she couldn't be sure. Anyway, she was thankful that the young man hadn't been burned alive as she wouldn't have wanted his death on her conscience.

I could hear her heart thumping away as she thought about it, and the bosom of the deep rose and fell awfully.

John Diamond had been put to bed upstairs and Dr. Fisher from Hertford had been with him for about half an hour, and so had Mrs. Small who kept coming and going and saying things about raw meat.

"Ssh! Mrs. Small! Little pitchers!"

"Ain't he asleep then?"

"He keeps waking."

"The crafty thing!"

Mr. Seed came over to have a look at me, and he twisted up his large face until he looked like Punch after he'd demolished Judy, the hangman, and Death.

"No more footsteps, Mr. Jones . . ."

"He's asleep, poor thing!"

"He'll be all right now," said Mrs. Small, who had mysteriously bandaged up my hands without my having been in the least aware of it.

My fingers, coming out of a nest of bandages, didn't look as if they belonged to me. In fact, they looked rather like toes.

"William, dear," said my mother.

"Now don't spoil him, Rose," said my Uncle Turner, as if I was in a state of precarious perfection that couldn't possibly last, and that any praise at all would ruin me.

"And how is our young hero?" said Dr. Fisher, who seemed to have come down through the ceiling.

My Uncle Turner looked daggers at him.

"He's asleep."

"Just as well. Nature knows best."

"I doubt that!" said Mr. K'Nee.

His voice sounded dry and sharp and his fistical face seemed to punch the air. "And how is the—the other one?"

"Not to be moved."

"Will he recover?"

"There's a good chance. He has everything to live for. His father, you know. I never saw such love between a father and son."

"It wasn't always like that."

"So I understand."

"Will it last?"

"God willing."

"I hope so. I don't want him to be disappointed. It would kill him."

"Kill who?" I said.

"Ssh! Ssh!"

"I want to know!"

"The old gentleman, dear. That's all. Mr. K'Nee was . . ."

"Is he asleep again, Mrs. Alice?"

"Like an angel, ma'am."

I hovered, with beating wings.

"I don't believe the young man could be so unnatural as to go back to his old ways," said my mother. "I just don't believe it, Mr. K'Nee."

"It wouldn't be unnatural, Mrs. David Jones," said the lawyer wearily. "Far from it. In my experience nature goes more easily to the bad than in any other direction. Wrong breeds wrong more readily than right breeds right."

"I don't agree with you, Mr. K'Nee!" said Mr. Seed abruptly. "I don't agree at all!"

"I'm surprised to hear you say that, Mr. Seed," said the lawyer coldly, as if he was annoyed to be contradicted by his own doorkeeper. "I'm very surprised to hear you, who work in Foxes Court and see a good deal of human nature, take such a kindly view of it."

"I'm sure there's good in everybody," said my mother. "It only needs bringing out."

"That's it, dear lady. It needs bringing out. And that's why we have the law. Leave it all to nature, and the bad flourishes like the bay tree."

"Very true," said my Uncle Turner, sensing an ally. "Particularly with boys."

"Leave one rotten apple in a barrel of sound ones," said Mr. K'Nee, ignoring my uncle, "and what happens? They all go bad. Put one good apple in a barrel of rotten ones, and what happens? Do the bad apples reform themselves? Do they become good? No. The good one goes to the bad with the rest."

"Ah! He's right!" sighed Mrs. Alice. "Apples is just like that!"

"Let me put it another way, Mrs. David Jones. It is natural, is it not, to take what you want . . . a loaf of bread, say. But it is not natural to pay for it. Yet pay we do, and pay we must. That is the law. And the law, ma'am, is the most unnatural thing in the world!

"What could be more unnatural than twelve good men and true deciding on the innocence or guilt of a perfect stranger? What could be more unnatural than a gentleman in a full-bottomed wig sentencing that stranger, who he's never seen in his life before, for a crime that can only have injured another total stranger?

"It's quite against nature, ma'am. And thank God for that! I tell you, if Mother Nature, with all her sloppy ways, was to come up at the Old Bailey, she'd be clapped into Newgate directly, and loaded with chains!"

Mr. K'Nee and his rotten apples went back to London after breakfast. He took Mr. Seed with him; but I wished he could have taken more. I wished he could have taken away everything he'd said about its being more natural for wrong to breed wrong than for right to breed right.

I knew he'd probably talked like that because he was frightened for his old friend and thought that the reconciliation might not last; but all the same, I wished he hadn't said it. It made the world seem a dark and gloomy place, with only lawyers to keep it from rotting away.

Mr. Seed would have stayed, but the claims of Hanging Sword Alley were too strong. It was his duty to preside over the Christmas Dinner; and Mrs. Branch would be expecting him for soup.

I asked him to give my best wishes to her and to all the Carwardines, and to thank them for their great kindness. I left out Mrs. Baynim on purpose as I felt that nothing I could say would do any good in that quarter.

"If you should be passing," said the dwarf, noting down my requests with brisk nods of his head, "at any time at all, and have a mind to inspect your property, so to speak, you will be very welcome, Mr. Jones. You will be very welcome indeed. We will consider the matter of the eleven shillings and sixpence closed," he added magnanimously.

He was standing by the carriage and Mr. K'Nee was urging him to climb aboard.

"Coming, Mr. K'Nee. Coming directly!" And then to me, very solemnly: "No more footsteps, eh, young Mr. Jones? No more sighs."

He shook me carefully, by my bandaged hand; and, although his fingers ended where most people's began, I never noticed. It was as if I'd shaken hands with those finger thoughts of his.

Then he climbed up into the coach and it moved off and was soon lost among the trees.

That evening I went upstairs to see John Diamond. I didn't really want to, but it seemed to be expected of me. In fact it was old Mr. Diamond himself who suggested it.

I met Mrs. Small coming out of his room and she looked at me gauntly and told me not to stay long. I'd hoped she was going to forbid me to go in as I dreaded that I would see the old hatred still burning in his eyes.

But I needn't have worried. He kept them shut all the time, and Mrs. Small had bandaged him up so thoroughly that I might have been visiting a bolster with arms.

"Who is it? Who's there?"

"It's me. William Jones."

"Oh. Pardon me if I don't shake hands with you."

"That's all right."

Silence; and I wondered if I could go.

"My pa says you got burned too, William."

"It wasn't much. Only my hands."

Silence again; and I wondered how he managed to eat.

"It hurts, don't it, William!"

"Yes. But yours must be worse."

"I'll live!"

"I'm glad of that."

"Thank you . . . and—thank you again, if you know what I mean."

"That's all right."

Another silence; the longest of all.

"Merry Christmas, William Jones."

"Merry Christmas, John Diamond."

22

IT WAS ON THE FRIDAY after Christmas, in the middle of the night. We'd moved into the part of our house that was still standing, even though the bricks were scorched.

It was very strange, knowing that certain passages ended in nothing, and that, if you'd opened a door, you'd have fallen straight outside into a blackened ruin with the stars shining down through a skeleton roof.

I was in my Uncle Turner's room. He'd gone back to St. Albans, to shout and bang the table in my grandmother's house.

He'd had a terrible quarrel with my mother. Unfortunately I missed most of it so I'm not sure whether it was about my father or me, as, of course, he'd found out about what my father had done in the old days.

I remember him saying, in that loud, bullying voice of his, that he'd always warned my mother and now it was too late and he hoped she was sorry. My mother shouted back that she wasn't; and, what was more, was going to send him a bill for his keep.

My uncle gave a large sneer at this and said he'd expected as much as my mother could do with every penny she could lay her hands on as it was going to cost her a fortune to rebuild the house.

My mother said that, thank God, David had been a good husband to her and had left her a rich woman and she didn't want for anything. And that included my uncle.

My uncle bellowed that she wasn't rich and never had been and that easy circumstances was the most that could have been said; and that by the time the builders had finished she'd be practically a pauper.

"Do you know what it will cost, Rose? A fortune! And where will you find it? Growing on trees?"

Then my mother told him to keep his voice down or did he want all the neighborhood to hear? She had seen me.

But that didn't stop him and he went on to say that the neighborhood would know soon enough when my mother didn't have a crust of bread to bless herself with.

"*Will* you be quiet!" yelled my mother. "Can't you see the boy's there?"

"Ah!" said my uncle triumphantly. "If only you'd let me have him for six months—"

"Thank God I didn't!" said my mother. "Because then he'd have turned out like you!"

That was the last straw. Soon after my uncle left us. He went away in a state of purple indignation and a hired coach. I remember thinking as he went, quite unrepentant, that there really must be a Day of Judgment waiting at the end of the world for people like my Uncle Turner to wake up and see for themselves what pigs they were.

That was on the Friday after Christmas. Christmas itself was an odd, loose-leaf sort of day; by which I mean that it didn't seem to

fit in with the rest of the week, and seemed as if it was always going to come fluttering out on its own.

Chiefly it was because of Mrs. Small being at the inn where we
had our dinner. She didn't say much—above a whisper, that is—
but she certainly exerted an *influence*.

Even my mother was awed by her. I think this was because
Mrs. Small had been widowed three times to my mother's once,
and rather looked down on her as being a mere beginner.

She was always going up and down stairs with a jug of gravy. I
never found out what she did with it, just as I never found out why
she disliked leaves. She was a woman of many secrets.

Curiously enough she never saw the point of observing secrecy
in a game of cards; and when Mr. Diamond and his son tried to
play, and she held the cards for John as he couldn't manage them
for himself, she always told Mr. Diamond exactly what cards she
was holding, in a slow, earnest voice, and so spoiled the game. But
it didn't really matter as there weren't any stakes. Old Mr. Diamond and his son played for love.

On the day after Christmas there was an unexpected visitor to
the inn. It was Mr. K'Nee's clerk, Mr. Jenkins. Mr. K'Nee had
sent him down to Woodbury with some money for Mr. Diamond.

He went upstairs to see his old associate, but I don't know what
passed between them. With me, however, he was a much milder
Mr. Jenkins than I'd remembered. I don't say that he fawned, but
he'd certainly developed a habit of ducking his head whenever
anybody looked at him, as if that article had been clouted hard and
often in the recent past.

Afterwards Mr. Diamond told me that, although Mr. K'Nee
had threatened Mr. Jenkins with a hanging, he'd relented and con-

tinued to employ him on account of Mr. Jenkins having a widowed mother.

Mr. Jenkins himself said nothing about the letter he'd sent me and when I mentioned it he looked at me searchingly and asked if it had been signed.

"No," I said.

"Ah," said he. "Then it ain't a legal document, young feller-me-lad! Burn it!"

Before he left, he beckoned me to one side.

"That ten thousand pound," he murmured. "Did you ever find it?"

"There wasn't any money."

"Tell me another!" said he, tapping the side of his nose very sagaciously. "There's money all right. And it's somewhere!"

There was no shaking him in this, and when he went back to his owner in London, he left me thinking yet again of Mr. K'Nee's words that boys and fools are always dreaming of treasure. Well, I still dreamed a little, but I was a boy; but Mr. Jenkins wasn't, so there was no choice but to think of him as a fool.

So Christmas was over and there weren't even any presents as they'd all gone up in the fire; and it was Friday night and another year before it would be Christmas again.

The dwarf had told me that there wouldn't be any sighs or footsteps again. Well, he was wrong. There were sighs in my room; and they were mine. And there were footsteps, too; and they were mine. My father's ghost was at rest; but mine was wide awake.

Just as in teeming London there had been quiet courts enclosing fond remembrances of the country, so inside of me there was a court, only it enclosed a remembrance of the town. It beat and glittered and winked and shone, and not all the trees and fields and leafy lanes could put it out.

It was snowing outside; and I wondered if it was snowing in London, and if all the chimney pots were wearing white hats and looking as if they were going to be confirmed.

I turned away from the window and thought about what my uncle had said—about our being paupered when the builders had done; and I wondered if I could go on the snick-an-lurk to restore our fallen fortunes.

It must have been long after midnight when I looked out again. The snow had stopped and there was a thick white carpet all over the ground.

I remember I stared at it for some time before I noticed a very strange thing. There were footprints in the snow. And they'd only just been made.

They came from the gate in a wavering zigzag line. They missed the drive and went round the tree in the middle. Then they made a great loop and marched right across the front of the house.

My first idea was that it was Liverguts coming to murder me with his terrible hook. Even as I thought it, it seemed to be confirmed.

There was the most awful scream from right inside the house! It was Rebecca! A second later Cissy screamed; and then my mother who'd been sleeping in the room next to theirs! Shriek! Shriek! Shriek!

Then Mrs. Alice and the kitchen-maid! They went off like fireworks: shriek—shriek—shriek!

They were being murdered, not exactly in their beds, but out in the passage! They were all out there in their nightgowns. The kitchen-maid had a candle and she was shaking so much that the shadows were going mad, and Mrs. Alice had a broom.

My mother and my sisters were yelling their heads off and the only man in the house was me, as the gardener was living in the village on account of the stables having been burned. Feeling the importance of my situation, I advanced.

"Keep away, William! Keep away! I've got him!"

I saw there was something fearful crouching against the wall under the shadow of the broom. It was like a large hedgehog, with a strong suggestion of spikes and fleas.

"Ar!" said the hedgehog, making a sudden movement that caused the kitchen-maid to yelp and stagger so that all the shadows fled pell-mell up the wall. "There y'are, Willum! It's me!"

"Who is it? For God's sake, who is it?" moaned my mother, terrified and appalled that my name should have come out of the grisly object that seemed to have no face. "Who is it, William?"

"It's my friend," I said. "It's my friend, Shot-in-the-Head."

So they hadn't killed him after all! He'd got a terrible cut down the side of his neck from Liverguts's hook, and it looked as if it was going rotten. He'd got half of Hertfordshire in his hair, and the other half over his hands and face. His feet were coming out of his boots and he was coming out of everywhere else; and he stank of Whitefriars and Blackfriars and Shoreditch and the great Fleet Ditch. But he wasn't dead!

He stood up. He peered at my mother and sisters and then at Mrs. Alice and her broom. I thought he was going to screech and spit.

Instead he fished and fumbled deep inside himself and then, with a grunt of satisfaction, brought something out.

" 'Ere y'are," he said. "Real moccy leather, ain't it? Got it back orf Liverguts for yer."

It was my purse. It was the purse I'd thrown away in the Sun in Splendour. Shot-in-the-Head had remembered how I'd boasted about it and he'd got it back for me because I'd saved his life.

It was when I'd shouted "Boarders!" and brought all White-friars out that he'd got clean away. Or nearly clean, there being the little matter of the rent in his neck.

After that he'd found another doss and picked up his crumbs, as he put it, until he was strong enough to go once more on the snick-an-lurk.

Then, remembering all I'd told him about where I'd lived, he'd tramped all the way to come and pay me back. He'd have come a day sooner, but he'd taken a hundred wrong turnings among country lanes, which were worse than all the town put together; and even when he'd found the house, he'd gone into one wrong door after another and been greeted with shrieks. But it had come out all right in the end.

I wished Mr. K'Nee had been there. I really did. There hadn't been twelve good men and true who'd said that Shot-in-the-Head owed me anything; and there hadn't been a gentleman in a full-bottomed wig who'd sentenced him to pay me back. There'd been nobody but Shot-in-the-Head himself.

When he told us about his journey, I was pleased to see that Rebecca was crying; and even Cissy's eyes caught the candlelight like dew.

He slept that night with me; and next morning my mother

asked me if he had anywhere else to go. She asked quite gently but it was plain that she hoped he'd turn out to have dear friends somewhere else. I shook my head.

"He *is* the one who saved you, William? It's really him?"

I nodded; and my mother sighed and looked faintly reproachful, as if it was just like me to have picked on someone like Shot-in-the-Head to be saved by, instead of a wholesome, respectable boy you could take anywhere.

"Perhaps," I suggested helpfully, "we could send him to my Uncle Turner for six months. Then we wouldn't know him when he came back."

"Don't be ridiculous, William!" snapped my mother, who was still rather sensitive about that awful pig.

So there it is. It's April now and the Diamonds have long since gone back to Club Cottage with great plans and small smiles. The leaves are all out and the builders are in and I've told everybody that we're going to be paupers, which my mother says is nonsense and she doesn't want to hear me mention that again.

My friend is still with us, and I think he's going to stay. Of course he's been washed and looks rather unfamiliar. But it's Shot-in-the-Head all right, and his hair is the brightest of red.

Rebecca, plain, virtuous Rebecca of all people, has taken quite a liking to him, and, I've noticed, has begun to pick up some of his expressions; but she doesn't know what they mean.

For instance, he gave her a gold and ruby brooch that he'd brought away with him. Naturally, Cissy and my mother told her outright that she couldn't keep it as it was almost certainly stolen.

"It's not! It's not!" shouted Rebecca furiously. "He told me on his honor that he got it on the snick-an-lurk!"

I haven't told her what that means, yet. I'm saving it up for a rainy day.

My mother wants to call him Seth, as she says that Shot-in-the-Head isn't a name at all. Seth Jones, she says, has quite a ring to it. I don't like it and I don't think my friend does, either. I wouldn't mind calling him John, as I'd once thought that he *was* John—John Diamond, I mean—and had actually dreamed of his coming back to my home, just as he'd done.

But those were all old dreams; and there are new ones now. He still sleeps in my room and every night we talk and talk. We talk about treasure.

We've drawn a map of where his great treasure is still hidden, in the pockets of his roof house in Whitefriars. We think it's still there, unless the woman with the baby has found it and turned herself into a duchess.

We've marked the river and we've marked St. Paul's with a cross; and I've written over the parts where the murderers live. Whenever I look at it, I think that it looks like a dream map of pirates' gold.

But it's real. Boys and fools, Mr. K'Nee had said, always dream of treasure. Well, there really is one. I promise you that; and I know where it is.